How was a gi
marry and have
cowboys of Mule Hollow wouldn't ask her out?

Except for *him,* Dan Dawson…a notorious flirt who asked everyone out.

"You know, Ashby, I could help you. I mean, I could help you find a husband."

She almost tripped. "Excuse me?" *Could this day get any worse?*

"I know what your problem is." He shrugged.

That brought her up short. "My problem?" she gritted through clenched teeth.

He grinned, then winked. Dan Dawson and winking was a lethal combination. Ashby might be immune to Dan's shallow charm, but she wasn't dead.

"Ash, you know what I'm talking about—you keep refusing to go out with me."

"I'm looking for a man who wants to get married. We both know that isn't you."

Books by Debra Clopton

Love Inspired

**The Trouble with Lacy Brown* #318
**And Baby Makes Five* #346
**No Place Like Home* #365
**Dream a Little Dream* #386
**Meeting Her Match* #402
**Operation: Married by Christmas* #418
**Next Door Daddy* #428
**Her Baby Dreams* #440

*Mule Hollow

DEBRA CLOPTON

was a 2004 Golden Heart finalist in the inspirational category, a 2006 Inspirational Readers' Choice award winner, a 2007 Golden Quill award winner and a finalist in the 2007 American Christian Fiction Writers Book of the Year. She praises the Lord each time someone votes for one of her books, and takes it as an affirmation that she is exactly where God wants her to be.

Debra is a hopeless romantic and loves to create stories with lively heroines and the strong heroes who fall in love with them. But most importantly, she loves showing her characters living their faith and seeking God's will in their lives one day at a time. Her goal is to give her readers an entertaining story that will make them smile, hopefully laugh and always feel God's goodness as they read her books. She has found the perfect home for her stories writing for Love Inspired and still has to pinch herself just to see if she really is awake and living her dream.

When she isn't writing Debra enjoys taking road trips, reading and spending time with her two sons, Chase and Kris. She loves hearing from readers and can be reached through her Web site, debraclopton.com, or at P.O. Box 1125, Madisonville, Texas 77864.

Her Baby Dreams

Debra Clopton

Published by Steeple Hill Books™

STEEPLE HILL BOOKS

Steeple Hill®

ISBN-13: 978-0-373-87476-7
ISBN-10: 0-373-87476-6

HER BABY DREAMS

This edition published by arrangement with Steeple Hill Books.

www.SteepleHill.com

Printed in U.S.A.

What does the Lord require of you? To act justly and to love mercy and to walk humbly with your God.

—*Micah* 6:8

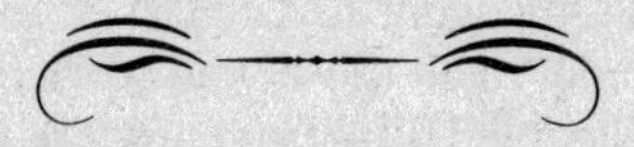

To Heidi Clopton my very first and dearly loved daughter-in-law. You are a jewel!

Special thanks and acknowledgments go to editorial assistant Elizabeth Mazer for all you do in the process of getting my books ready for the readers; to my agent Joyce Hart, who is always there for me; to all those who work behind the scenes at Steeple Hill—from artwork to shipping and everything in between, your efforts are greatly appreciated. Most important, special thanks to my gifted editor Krista Stroever for your honesty, tireless hard work and inspiration.

Chapter One

"Come on, Ash, just climb up here and we'll be on our way." Dan Dawson patted the handlebars and grinned at her with that mesmerizing smile of his, and expected that to be enough.

Ashby Templeton stared across the now dusty bicycle at the too-handsome-for-his-own-good cowboy, and wondered what terrible, horrible deed she'd done to deserve this kind of punishment.

The cowboy fully expected that just because he asked with a smile, she would comply!

Arms crossed, she held her ground. Despite the power of that smile, she was not going to climb up there to teeter precariously as he pedaled the bike. It had nothing to do with being difficult. It had to do with ability. She just couldn't do it.

Far too used to getting his own way with those midnight-blue eyes, Dan batted them once more while patting the bars again. "We're losing, Ash. Why did you sign up for this race if you weren't going to cooperate?"

She wasn't ready to answer that, either. This left her with a blank stare as her only defense against the cocky slant of his smile. Dangerous stuff for anyone to witness. Still, she held her ground.

"It's supposed to be a fun race, done as a team," he continued. "That means one of us has to ride and one of us has to pedal. C'mon, hop on now and we can still make a decent showing. Haven't you ever seen *Butch Cassidy and the Sundance Kid?*"

Feeling the sting of humiliation, Ashby stalked away from him down the country road, wishing with all her might that she'd had a normal upbringing. *This!* This *fiasco* was her blue-blooded mother's fault.

Ashby could not tell Dan Dawson that in her world, knowing how to host a dinner party was considered "essential" information. Riding a bike was something the gardening crew did to get to work. She had to say something, though. She spun toward him, met his gaze and knew she would rather limp barefoot and bleeding across that finish line than admit the truth.

A slight exaggeration, but still, she could not tell him. He arched a brow, waiting for her reply. More humiliation tangled inside her.

"If we're going to finish at all, then we'd better stop talking and get moving," she huffed. "I told you in town that I was going to walk. Walking *together* is a team effort, too." She started walking again.

Fifteen feet farther on, hearing no sound behind her, Ashby could only assume he was standing in the middle of the road watching her, waiting for her to give in.

"This is just ridiculous," he muttered at last, and rode up beside her within seconds. "What is the big deal? The other gals hopped up on those handlebars like good sports. That's why when Applegate shot the starting gun, they tore out of there like good competitors do, and left us in their dust. That's why everyone was laughing when you headed out at a fast trot behind them."

"I did not *trot.*" She felt guilty about all that, but really, there was no need to get ugly. It wasn't her fault that this truly was all she could do. How could she tell him that she couldn't ride a bike? How could she admit that the very thought of climbing onto a bike flustered her so that she got this confounded vertigo? She glanced at him in her peripheral vision and picked up the pace. Trot, my foot!

He looped around ahead of her on the blacktop and came back toward her like a circling vulture.

"So why *did* you sign up?" He intercepted her gaze as he went by. "This was supposed to be a boy meets girl, girl meets the man of her dreams shindig. At least, that's what I thought."

"Man of her dreams—boy, they got that one wrong," Ashby grumbled under her breath.

"What's that?" He swooped around her, holding his legs out, his boot tips pointing straight up to the sky.... The cowboy was in a bike race wearing jeans, boots and a Stetson! And if she weren't so put out by all of this, she'd say it was a little bit cute. Some of the other cowboys had forgone their standard uniform in favor of shorts. Their legs were as white as the silk wedding dress hanging in the window of her dress shop. Even so, they were probably far more comfortable than Dan, though he hadn't even broken a sweat. Not so for her... It just wasn't fair any way you looked at it.

She pulled a wayward strand of hair off her damp cheek and focused on what was really bothering her.

The vertigo.

"C'mon, Ash, spit it out. Why did you sign up?"

"I *didn't* sign up," she snapped, regretting it even as the words erupted from her lips.

"Ha! I was right." He jerked the handlebars and again swooped back in her direction. "When the ladies announced they were adding this couples' bike race to the spring festival, I told all the boys there was no way you'd be signing up for it. Of course, nobody disagreed with me."

"What?" It was Ashby's turn to twirl around to stare at him as he made the loop behind her. The world spun drunkenly, but she took a deep breath and let it settle down, while he continued as if he hadn't noticed that her voice dripped with indignation.

"Yup. Imagine our surprise when you walked out there and got in the lineup."

A knot formed in the pit of her stomach at Dan's disheartening revelation. *The cowboys hadn't thought she would participate.* They'd all automatically assumed she wouldn't.

How could they presume such a thing? She'd moved to Mule Hollow almost a year ago specifically to find a husband. True, it wasn't as if she was shouting it to the treetops. But this was a town that had advertised for wives for all the bachelors, so of course she'd expected that the cowboys knew any single girl moving in had hopes of marrying.

She swallowed, fighting to keep her expression neutral. She didn't want Dan Dawson to have the satisfaction of knowing how deeply that remark hurt. There was absolutely no one who could want a baby more than she did. Want a warm, nurturing, lovable family. A family that would go on picnics together, that wouldn't be afraid to get down in the grass and roll around if the notion struck. A family who would learn to ride bikes together...every last one of them. Of course, before she could ride bikes with her children, she was going to have to learn herself.

Ashby breathed through her nose and tried to regain her control. But it was hard, when all she could think about was that she was almost thirty years old. *Thirty.* That meant her biological clock was ticking on an accelerated timetable, and things were not looking good for the family she wanted so much.

How was a girl supposed to marry and have babies when the cowboys of Mule Hollow wouldn't ask her out?

Except for *him,* Dan Dawson...a notorious flirt who asked everyone out. Her "friends" were definitely playing mud ball here. What could have possessed them to partner her up with him? It just didn't make sense. They knew how much she wanted to settle down.

Sweat ran down her face and she pushed more hair off her sticky skin. Her mood deteriorated further as she watched Dan glide by again.

He made it look so easy.

Riding a bike, that is. As he got a little way ahead of her he let go and effortlessly pedaled down the yellow stripe, no hands.

Ashby walked faster. She would have jogged a little, except—well, there was that dizziness and the blister growing on her heel. And, well, she'd never been much of an athlete. Her mother hadn't encouraged it when Ashby was growing up. She'd spent most of her days in frilly pastel dresses, sitting primly at one endless function after another. Ashby had learned to despise her blue blood long before she even knew what it was. She had actually forgotten until today that there had been a time when she'd really wanted to learn to ride a bicycle.

Dan circled back, and a picture of her as a child holding her nanny's hand in Golden Gate Park watching other kids riding by flashed through her memory. She in her frills and patent leather Mary Janes.

"You know, Ashby, I could help you."

She blinked hard and focused on the red ribbon off in the distance, signaling the route back toward town and the finish line of this five-mile nightmare.

"I'm almost afraid to ask what you mean," she said. How long had they been out here? She checked her watch—just over an hour! It felt like days.

"I mean, I could help you find a husband."

She almost tripped. "Excuse me?" Could this day get any worse?

"Hey, I'm good at reading people. I can usually tell what someone needs."

She gave him the evil eye, clamping her mouth firmly shut. Why couldn't a rabbit hole open up right then and there?

He shrugged. "I know what your problem is."

That brought her up short. "My problem?" she said through gritted teeth.

He grinned, then winked.

Dan Dawson and winking was a lethal combination. He already looked better than any man alive had a right to. Add a wink… Ashby might be immune to Dan's shallow charm, but she wasn't dead.

She sucked in a couple of deep breaths as he pedaled slowly beside her.

"Ash, you know what I'm talking about. I have been trying to help you out for a year now. But how am I going to do that if you keep refusing to go out with me? You should give me points for persistence."

"Hardly. Besides, how is going out with you supposed to help me? I'm looking for a man who wants to get married." *Going out with you would be a complete waste of time I don't have,* she almost said, but it sounded too harsh. Instead, she took a more diplomatic approach. "We both know that isn't you."

"But it would be fun."

"And that is my point," she huffed, dragging to a halt. "Why would I want to go out with you just to have fun?"

He stopped riding. "See, that right there. That is exactly what I'm talking about."

She did not get this man.

"You need to loosen up, Ash. Live a little! You are never going to get a date if you don't. Even a lonesome cowboy isn't desperate enough to marry a gal so knotted up she can't have a good time."

"I…" Ashby swallowed hard, forcing herself to hold his gaze. "I can have a good time."

He patted the handlebars, challenge in his eyes. "Show me."

"No." She refused to be goaded into trying something she would regret. Anyway, when she fell flat on her face, it would only add lack of balance to her apparently well-documented list of shortcomings.

No way. She resumed walking. Stalking, actually. Stalking wasn't good. It made her far more aware of how much her feet were killing her. She was having to fight the urge to limp, and was afraid to think about the size of the blister that was building….

To her surprise, Dan hopped off the bike and started walking beside her, pushing it between them. "You are a puzzle, Ashby Templeton. Yes, indeedy, a real jigsaw."

Ashby lifted her chin and didn't take the bait.

"Does it get lonesome up there?"

She cut her eyes toward him. "Up where?"

"On that high horse you ride."

"I don't ri—" She glared at him.

"No use denying it." He reached across the bike and pulled a piece of wet hair off her cheek.

To Ashby's horror, her pulse went ballistic. She stepped away from him and the bad choices he represented. Their rejections because she wasn't "good enough" still stung, but she had a major weakness for bad choices. Brad. Carlton. Steven… She'd been such a fool. Wasted so many years. But no more. "Look," she said, glaring at Dan. "I have no problem with you hopping on that bike and riding off into the sunset. I'd welcome it, actually." Yes, she would.

"Nope, wouldn't be right. If you're going to insist on walking, then I walk, too."

Ashby dug deep for clarity. Focused on her friends. Friends who had better run the other way when they saw her coming. She might have been brought up to be a lady: calm, cool and collected—but even a lady had her breaking point.

Chapter Two

Dan had never met a more bullheaded woman. Ashby beat the competition hands down.

He slid her a glance. It was obvious her feet were killing her. Her pace had slowed over time, and when she thought he wasn't watching, she was limping on her right foot. Crazy woman.

So get on the bike already and let him do the work. *What,* he wanted to shout out, *was the big deal?*

He took a deep breath. The woman had a way of getting under his skin, and had from the first day they'd met. He could count on his left thumb the number of women who'd ever turned him down for a date. That woman was limping stubbornly beside him right now.

"Look, I know your feet are killing you."

She scorched him with a glare that warmed his blood. Yanking the bike to a halt, he watched her increase the distance between them. Yes, sir, there she went with her perfectly blunt-cut hair swinging and swaying in perfect time with each step she took. Everything about her was perfect.

Which was precisely her problem. She was just too perfect.

Still, did she honestly think she was too good to ride on the handlebars of his bike? When he'd signed up, he'd been expecting to draw some high-spirited gal as a partner, and spend a pleasant afternoon on this little escapade. Boy, was the laugh on him.

Could Ashby not see the potential in the whole game?

Standing in the center of the blacktop, exactly halfway along the course, he watched her struggle.

It just didn't make sense. None of it. Not the limping, or the refusal to get on the stinkin' bike. He ought to throw her over his shoulder and haul her into town kicking and screaming.

But that wasn't his way. He hung his head and gathered his wits as he tried to come up with a new strategy. One that didn't require losing his temper, since he didn't allow himself to lose his temper, ever. Especially with a female. He refused to follow in his father's footsteps.

But the woman was hurting herself for no good reason.

He shouldn't be surprised. She'd been Miss Prim from the moment she'd first shown up in Mule Hollow. Beyond perfect, like an airbrushed cover girl. Most of the cowboys around town had taken one look at her and figured she was out of their league.

Dan, never one to be accused of a lack of confidence,

thought he'd do her a favor and break the ice, so he'd asked her out. Maybe that way the other wranglers would see she was approachable.

He'd just been trying to help her out.

Imagine his surprise when the woman turned him down. One flat no, and she'd sashayed off, high heels clicking on the plank sidewalk.

Worst part of the scenario was that this had taken place in front of Sam's Diner, with a herd of cowboys watching from the shadows inside.

The very idea that she'd refused to go out with him sparked a challenge in Dan. He'd decided right then and there he was going to get a date with her if it took a year. It was the principle of the whole thing.

Of course that was before he'd realized the ramifications of their interaction.

Little did she know it, but she'd sealed her fate that day. He felt bad about the fact that asking her out in public had backfired as it had. Dan had been kidded and teased no end, because of the brutal way she'd shot him down. He could feel sorry for himself, but a little teasing never hurt anyone. Then again, he suspected Ashby wouldn't feel the same way. This woman was all business when it came to dating. It was all about finding a husband. She had no idea that because of that day in front of Sam's, unless something drastic happened, she was done. When a cowpoke got turned down by a gal, the slang expressions in certain cowboy circles was no longer that he'd gotten axed, but that he'd been "Ashed."

Of course, to the fellas it was harmless joking.

If her reaction just now was any indication, she'd explode if she knew what was being said. Dan really felt guilty about the whole thing. He'd thought asking her out in public would break the ice, not shut her down.

For a natural fixer like him, that was hard to deal with. As a boy whose earliest memories were of his mother getting smacked around by his dad, the need to fix situations had become embedded in his emotional makeup. His approach to problems was a talent he'd happened upon by accident a few years later, living in a women's shelter with his mom. All the occupants of which, like his mother, needed their confidence rebuilt.

He'd learned that when he smiled, women smiled.

It had first happened when he tried to make his mom feel better, and saw that his smile brightened her expression. But when he'd seen his smile cause a young woman with a black eye and a swollen lip to smile back at him, it had dawned on even a kid of six that a little charm could transform someone's life. If only for a moment.

Dan had been blessed with a playful heart, and God had given him an unlikely path at an early age that he had followed into adulthood.

Things with Ashby weren't entirely the same. He couldn't explain it completely, but he'd unknowingly given her a bad rep, and he felt a need to repair it.

He'd tried telling the guys she'd been having a bad day but it had not convinced them. So he figured if she'd go out with him, like he'd planned originally, that it would redeem her in the eyes of the other cowboys.

Not so easy. She wasn't cooperating for some reason. Despite this, they'd actually developed a relationship based on banter over the months of continued rejection—banter he found entertaining most of the time. Not today.

This day was going to add to the urban legend she'd become, and try as he might, there was nothing he could do.

Shaking his head, he pushed the bike forward. She didn't have a clue this race could very well seal her fate for good.

Unless she changed her ways, Ashby Templeton would die an old maid here in Mule Hollow, surrounded by cowboys diligently searching for wives. And she wouldn't even know why.

On Friday, Ashby walked into Heavenly Inspirations Salon knowing that something had to change. She just didn't know what.

Was she the reason that her love life was nonexistent?

She still hadn't completely forgiven her friends for setting her up in that horrible bike race with Dan Dawson two weeks earlier. What had they been thinking? It would go down in history as one of the worst days of her life. Honestly, they knew he was a thorn in her side. That she'd refused to go out with him several times over the past year. So why had they done it?

She'd told herself they'd acted with the best of intentions, however misguided they might be. Still, as she entered the salon, she could only shake her head that they were scraping the bottom of the barrel in an attempt to help her find a husband. They must really think her hopeless.

Lacy had called a meeting of the local ladies to discuss plans to attract more visitors to town.

"Hi, everyone," Ashby said, scanning the full room. The matchmakers were all present. Norma Sue Jenkins, robust and good-hearted, grinned at her from where she and redheaded Esther Mae Wilcox were shelling peas in the corner. Adela, their partner in matchmaking, was sitting at the manicure table watching Sheri, co-owner of the salon, paint her own toenails.

It had been Adela who'd come up with the idea to transform her small town into a place that would attract and hopefully hold a generation of younger women. They'd hatched their "wives wanted" ad campaign, and had been matchmaking ever since. Lacy had come along first and opened her salon; others soon followed. Still more came to the festivals and weekend events held to mingle with the cowboys and enjoy the imaginative, sometimes outrageous things this group came up with for them to participate in. The bike race being a case in point. Today, feeling dread like a lead ball in the pit of her stomach, Ashby wondered what new idea was brewing.

"Hey, Ashby, you do *not* look so good," Lacy said,

sitting in the shampoo chair, thumbing through a salon supply brochure.

"You sure don't," Sheri agreed.

The room grew still as everyone paused and stared. "I'm fine," Ashby said, and sat down in the chair by the door.

"You're not still upset about the spring festival, are you?" Esther Mae asked. "I just can't believe you didn't let that cutie-pie Dan give you a ride on the bike. That was the whole reason for the race. Why, me and my Hank used to love to ride around like that."

"Leave her be, Esther Mae. She must have had her reasons," Norma Sue said, adding dryly, "though not any I can figure out."

So much for the support, Ashby thought as Norma Sue eyeballed her.

"On the other hand," she added, "that was supposed to be an enjoyable adventure. I never in all of my days saw a person look as gloomy as you did when you limped into town."

"She had her reasons," Adela said, and Ashby gave her a grateful smile.

"I'm sorry I disappointed all of you. But the point is, I should never have been in that race. Especially paired up with Dan—"

"But the man is perfect for you."

Ashby stared at Esther Mae, too mystified by the observation to even gather a coherent defense. Her blood pressure escalated just thinking about him.

Esther Mae snapped a handful of pea pods in half as if to punctuate her shocking statement. "You should ask Dan out on a date."

Ashby's mouth fell open and chuckles erupted from every corner of the room.

"First off," she managed to reply, "I would never ask a man out on a date. And second, if I did, it certainly wouldn't be Dan."

"Well, I just don't understand you," Esther Mae said. "He is such a sweet boy."

"He's shallow and irresponsible," Ashby countered. She wanted to tell them she'd had the misfortune of being drawn to his kind, but she couldn't bring herself to shine that light on her failures. It wasn't easy telling others that the man she'd trusted and believed in had betrayed her. It was humiliating enough. Besides, she'd learned her lesson well. Flirts couldn't be trusted. Men like Steven… She pushed him from her thoughts. She didn't like thinking back. Instead she focused on Dan. "He flirts with everyone. It's as if he thinks that flashing that gorgeous smile of his will have women eating out of his hand!"

"It is a gorgeous smile," Esther Mae said. "Swashbuckling pirate. That's what I think when he flashes it."

Ashby felt heat flush her cheeks at the picture Esther Mae painted. "Why in the world would all of you think he and I could be more than antagonists? I frustrate him and he irritates me."

Esther Mae harrumphed. "You can't tell me you aren't attracted to him—"

"Esther Mae," Norma Sue said. "Leave the girl be. She just doesn't see it yet."

Ashby could see fine. It appeared they were the ones in need of an eye exam…or maybe a head exam. "Dan Dawson is not husband material," she said. This was the very group of ladies she'd hoped would help her find a mate, and it was very disconcerting to realize how off base they were. It was a discouraging blow to know that she was on her own, a situation that had never worked out before. She could not trust her own judgment when it came to men. She was afraid to. She'd believed in Steven and she never saw his betrayal coming. She needed help, but even God seemed to have decided to be silent on this issue.

"You don't have the right impression of Dan," Norma Sue said, drawing Ashby back from her morose thoughts.

"You certainly don't," Esther Mae agreed. "Exactly our reasoning behind tweaking the bike race so y'all would be together. Never underestimate the power of sparks."

Lacy waved her hands. "Okay, enough picking on Ashby. We called you down here to get your opinion on my new idea. You know we have a rodeo coming up in a couple of weeks, and we've been racking our brains for a new fund-raiser. The proceeds are going into the emergency fund for the shelter."

Ashby looked at them with leery eyes. "It doesn't involve me, bikes or Dan Dawson, does it?"

"Only if you want it to." Lacy chuckled. "It's a pig scramble."

Everyone but Ashby squealed in obvious delight at the very thought of such a thing.

She slowly scanned the room. "Could you elaborate on the term 'pig scramble'? Remember, I'm not a country girl."

Lacy's expertly shagged hair did a jig with her laughter. "It's where we grease up a small pig, let it loose in the arena, and whoever catches it wins the scramble. Doesn't that sound like a hoot and a half?"

Oh, Ashby got it. They were playing a joke on her; that's what this was all about. They were all waiting to see her reaction, before telling her their real idea. But a closer look at their expressions confirmed that they weren't joking.

Mule Hollow was about to have itself a pig scramble.

The expectant expressions surrounding her gave Ashby a bad feeling. "Oh no! Don't even think about conning me into this like you did that bike race," she said. "The day I scramble for a pig will be the day pigs fly!"

That killed them. Lacy and Sheri especially got so tickled that Ashby felt insulted. "Why the hysterical laughter?" she asked.

Sheri fanned herself. "Don't be silly. We knew you wouldn't scramble for a pig. The very idea is hilarious. We just wanted you to help us raise the donations. You have such a mind for business, we thought we'd run it by you, is all."

Ashby vaguely heard the last part of what Sheri said. "How did you know I wouldn't scramble for a pig?"

Sheri didn't even bat an eye. "I told them you wouldn't ride on the handlebars of a bike, and I was right. If you won't join the rest of us when we look silly doing something like that, then it doesn't take a genius to know you're not going to get down and dirty in the mud with a pig. No matter how much of a blast it'll be."

Lacy winced almost apologetically. "Especially since it is going to be a spectator sport. You know none of the guys would miss something like this."

There was actually a hint of a dare in Lacy's words. *Trap ahead* was ringing in Ashby's brain, but she ignored it. Why? Because nothing bothered her nearly as much as what Sheri had just said. Ashby had an instant visual of the smug little group of cowboys, including Dan Dawson, discussing who would and who wouldn't get in the pen with a pig.

Even a lonesome cowboy isn't desperate enough to marry a gal so knotted up she can't have fun. Dan's words had been playing in her head like a broken record over the last couple of weeks. *Knotted up...* Yes, she knew she was. She also knew that this was her chance to get unknotted once and for all. Her mother would cringe at her word choice. "So what does one have to do to get in this pig scramble?" Did she just ask that?

"Well, this is what we thought," Lacy said. "There's going to be so many gals wanting to get in that arena they won't all fit. We think it would be great to make the entry a competition. The ten gals who sell the most tickets and raise the most money get the privilege of scrambling for the pig. What do you think?"

"I'm determined to be one," Sheri said, with a gleam in her eyes. "I've never done it, but me and piggy have a date, and he's going down for the count."

"I'm with you, sister!" Lacy slapped palms with Sheri.

Ashby bit her lip and watched their display of enthusiasm. Ashby had never in her life high-fived anyone, and honestly, she wasn't feeling the urge at the moment.

"Pig scrambles are fun," Norma Sue said. "Me and Esther Mae tackled a few in our time."

"They're rough little cooters, though," Esther said.

Ashby's stomach felt sort of sick, but she knew she had to speak up. "Can I ask all of you something?"

"Shoot," Lacy said, fists on her hips.

This would be embarrassing, but she needed to know the truth. "Dan said that I couldn't get a date because the cowboys think I'm…well, *knotted up* was the phrase he used."

It was as if someone hit the mute button. Everyone in the room instantly clammed up and wouldn't look her in the eye. That was her clue—they knew something about this.

"Well," Lacy hedged. "We had heard something to that effect."

"This is horrible." Ashby wrung her hands. "And you didn't say anything. All this time—"

"No, now don't get all upset," Lacy said, crossing the room to place a comforting hand on her arm. "They just don't know you, Ashby. They don't know the caring and wonderful person you are, because all they can see is the perfect package that God put you in."

A chorus of agreement rang out around the room.

"I hate it when someone tells me how perfect I am," Ashby groaned. "I'm horrible at physical things. I'm like a gangly giraffe." And that was only appearancewise.

"Now, that is not true," Adela said, finally speaking up. "When you arrived here last year for the first spring festival, I seem to recall that you and the sheriff won the three-legged race."

"Only because Sheriff Brady was strong enough to haul me across the finish line. It had nothing at all to do with me."

"It's okay. Don't sweat it," Sheri said. "There is a guy out there for you, and when it's time for the two of you to meet, you will."

"Yes, but then it might be too late."

"Too late for what?" Adela asked.

"For me to have a baby."

Lacy cocked her head to the side. "Ashby, for goodness' sake, you're not even thirty."

"You're just a babe in the woods," Norma Sue said.

"Ha. At the pace I'm going…"

Lacy grinned. "Relax, girl. If there is one thing that history has taught us, it's that it is never, *never* too late. If God let Sarah have a baby at almost a hundred, you have to believe that if you are to have a baby, it will happen."

Ashby sighed again. "But will I be a hundred?"

"Ashby, listen to me," Sheri said. There wasn't a twinkle anywhere to be seen in her eyes as she leveled them on Ashby. "You may have to take the bull by the horns in order to make your dreams come true."

"That's right." Esther Mae shook her handful of pea pods for emphasis. "Empower yourself."

Ashby expelled an exasperated breath. "I thought I did. I moved all the way out here to Mule Hollow, but nothing has changed. The only man who has asked me out is a shallow playboy, whom all of you for some reason think is a good match for me."

"First of all," Sheri said, "I do think you have Dan all wrong. And second, you changed your zip code. You didn't change yourself."

Leave it to Sheri to be frank. Ashby felt the sting of her words all the way to her toes. "So you think I *am* stuck-up. You think they're right about me?"

"No." Lacy jumped in. "That's not what Sheri's saying."

"It certainly isn't. I think you are afraid. Believe me, I've been there. I think you are afraid of looking silly."

"He said that, too."

"Who, Dan?" Lacy asked.

Ashby nodded, feeling like a loser.

"Is it true?" Sheri asked.

"In a way. I was brought up in a setting where looking silly was the cardinal sin. I'm not sure I can do it. Really, that first day here, I thought I could, so when Brady grabbed me to be in the three-legged race with him, I did it. But when it was over I just couldn't stop thinking about how foolish I'd looked. Don't get me wrong, I love my mother, but I can't seem to get her voice out of my head." Now they probably all thought she was an awful person. Her relationship with her mother was complicated, but she did love her....

No-nonsense Sheri shook her head. "There comes a time when you make your own way in the world, Ashby. Totally and completely separate from your past. Even your mother. It's the only way to truly know who you are. What I found out as an adult is that my life is between me and the Lord."

Echoes of agreement rang out across the room.

"You would have had a blast riding those handlebars," Sherri continued. "And you could have a blast chasing a pig, too. Don't relegate yourself to the corner just because you don't have the best hand-eye coordination or because you think acting or looking silly is wrong. You have to laugh at yourself, take chances. Boy, did I ever learn that." She frowned. "Not that I meant to preach to you or anything. It just hit a nerve."

"Sheri's right," Lacy said. "If these cowboys see you out there laughing at yourself, they're going to start seeing the Ashby we know. The one who would make a great wife and mother...and who's one brilliant businesswoman."

"That's right," Norma Sue called out. Esther Mae and Adela were nodding and smiling in vigorous agreement.

Ashby fought back the lump that had lodged in her

throat. "I wish it were that simple." She thought about the bike. She'd always wanted to ride a bicycle. What about scrambling for a pig? Could she? Dan Dawson would say no. "So you really think me getting into that arena and trying to catch that pig might help me get a husband?"

Sheri and Lacy nodded like bobble heads.

Ashby inhaled sharply. "Okay." She had to do this. Even though her mother would be appalled at the idea.... Ashby had lived with the fear of a reporter saying the wrong thing about her in the Nob Hill or Pacific Heights society pages. Laughable, since her parents hadn't ever been considered elite enough to be newsworthy themselves. This was, however, Ashby had realized, one reason her mother was so preoccupied with fitting in with the upper crust. She lived, breathed and dreamed of the days when she or Ashby would be mentioned on the right pages of the right papers. This was why Ashby had let herself be pushed into dating first Brad and then Carlton. Both were highly newsworthy—and both had passed her over for more compatible matches for their blue money within the space of six months. Her mother had not been happy with Ashby on either count. To her way of thinking, Ashby had "lost" them deliberately.

Ashby hadn't dated again until after she'd moved away from home in San Francisco and opened her store in San Moreno, where she'd met Steven. Brad's and Carlton's rejection had devastated her mom. Steven's rejection had devastated Ashby. It was time to make a change.

Taking a deep, calming breath, she let the idea sink in. She took courage from everyone's smiles. "I'm probably going to be the laughingstock of Mule Hollow. But I'm in. I'm going to show certain people that I *can* loosen up." She gulped a very unladylike gulp.

She—Ashby Renee Templeton, who had never even played in a sandbox, much less in dirt—had a date with a *pig!*

Imagine that.

Chapter Three

The rodeo had been a good one, but it was about to get better. Leaning against the steel bars of the arena, Dan watched the group of laughing women prepare to do battle with the squealing pig in the pen behind him.

When he'd first learned that Ashby was going to participate, he figured it might be another train wreck. She'd been heavy on his mind in the month since they'd walked or limped the bike into town. Ashby had not been able to hide the pain of her blisters by the end of the disastrous ordeal. The cantankerous woman had refused all his attempts to help, and he'd finally stopped trying. Fortunately, by the time they'd made it into town, almost everyone was off participating in other festivities, sparing them some of the hoopla associated with coming in dead last.

Dan had to hand it to her, she'd said she wasn't riding the bike and she'd stuck to her guns. Blisters and all.

It stood to reason that when word spread of her raising money to win herself a spot in the scramble, there had been a stampede of cowboys lining up to help her along. The chance to support a worthy cause and see Ashby pitted against a pig had been too good to pass up for some people.

Not that she'd let Dan help her out. Oh, no, she'd *refused* to sell him a ticket.

Yup, she was still miffed at him.

Watching her now, he decided she looked stiff and nervous. He had to admit, though, that she looked nice, as usual. But his attention fixed on her luminous eyes, wide with trepidation.

His gut twisted. Those eyes should be wide with anticipation. He wanted her to relax and have a good time.

Not that she'd believe him.

Her back was as rigid as a ruler as she waited for the signal to enter the arena. Much like it had been every time she'd seen him over the past month.

Sunday school had been awkward, but he'd refrained from teasing her, not wanting to add to her dilemma. The one she had no idea she had. He'd tried to get the guys to stop with the "Ashed" nonsense, but his efforts had only drawn more attention to her plight. He had hopes for her tonight.

Tonight she might redeem herself. Tonight Miss Prim might just change her situation.

He hoped so. He didn't like feeling guilty.

Dan knew Roy Don Jenkins's voice was going to crack to life over the loudspeaker any minute now to introduce the women so he hurried to wish the ladies good luck before going back up to claim a seat in the stands. There were ten women in the group. Some were married; some were single; all had worked hard selling tickets to get into this arena. He admired the hard work they'd put into raising money that would help support the women's shelter. If a gal was ever curious about the way to his heart, that was it—donating time or money to women in need.

Not that he'd ever tell someone that bit of info; there were some things too private to talk about. Still, he'd come to wish them luck, and in doing so, silently thank them for their hard work and good hearts. "Ladies," he said, drawing their attention. "I just wanted to wish each and every one of you luck out there. Stay safe."

"Thanks, Dan," Lacy shouted over a sudden squawk of the amplifier.

Ashby jumped at the sound and her gaze connected with Dan's. Maybe she'd learn a thing or two from tonight. Even so, he hoped she wouldn't get hurt. As he went to find a seat in the stands, he sent up a prayer that they'd all be safe. It hadn't occurred to him until now that he'd sort of goaded her into this, and if she did get hurt, he'd be responsible. That was one burden he didn't care to take on.

She'd lost her mind. That was the first thought that hit Ashby as she and the others jogged out into the arena. The crowd roared with laughter. In front of her, Lacy and Sheri mugged and waved at the crowd, while she stumbled right into a wet spot and nearly went down.

Sheri laughed. "What are you trying to do—steal the show?"

Relieved to still be standing, Ashby glared at her. "You can have the show. I don't want to do this anymore."

"Sure you do," Lacy said.

Easy for her to say. Ashby wiped her damp palms on her jeans. The girl her mother raised wouldn't dare be caught dead in an arena, sweaty and hot, chasing after a greased pig! For an instant, all lingering animosity toward her upbringing disappeared as regret over her newfound rebellious streak assailed her.

Stop it.

Twenty feet away, the little animal squealed from behind the gate where they were holding him.

Ashby was about to tango with a pig.

Shifting nervously from foot to foot, she reminded herself that standing here in the arena was going to help not only the shelter, but also her image around town.

She glanced at Lacy, who was hunkered down like a linebacker ready for the tackle.

The pig squealed again, sounding like wet brakes on an overloaded bus! Ashby shivered. Who was she kidding? She was way out of her element!

Nothing to do but follow people who looked like they knew what they were doing. Mimicking Lacy, she shifted her weight from foot to foot, her elbows bent, hands out.

She just didn't have the personality to pull this off. Feeling foolish and out of place, she straightened and stood stiffly.

She was hopeless.

Roy Don called over the loudspeaker for the gate to open, and she almost jumped out of her skin when the pig shot into the arena in a frenzied panic.

And no wonder! Nine women reacted at once, squealing and laughing as they ran at poor Piggy en masse. This way and that the poor animal raced. When it suddenly froze, there was an instant pileup as everyone dived. Everyone, that is, but Ashby. She hadn't moved.

Nope. She was still standing exactly where she'd started. Maybe her slow reaction had saved her. Someone in that pileup had surely captured the pig.

Her dismay was huge when the slick pig squirted from the pile like a bar of soap in wet hands—just popped right out of there and…and headed *straight for her!*

Surely the charging pig could see that she was no threat. She was still frozen to the spot! Surely it understood that all it had to do was a bit of sidestepping and it would be home free. That the safety zone loomed only paces away.

But no, he couldn't know that. He was a pig. One with a vendetta, and who had decided to make like a bowling ball. After all, it had just taken down the nine other ladies, so why not Ashby?

Someone, somewhere, yelled for her to grab it.

Do what?

Grab it, her mind ordered.

Before she could analyze what she was doing, Ashby closed her eyes and dived.

That's right, she dived.

Straight for the forty pounds of squealing animal coming at her like greased lightning. She wasn't sure what astonished her the most, the fact that she voluntarily threw herself into the muck…

Or that she caught the pig!

She thought she heard the grandstands go wild, but the pig was screeching in her ear and kicking the wind out of her at the same time. One minute she had it, the next, Ashby was lying flat on her back as the slimy ball of lard used her as a launching pad. From her prone position, Ashby watched it shoot across the white line that had been drawn down the center of the arena. Pig: 1, Humans: 0.

Groaning, Ashby spat dirt and pushed herself up, grease and dirt embedded in her clothing. The slimy mixture of grime and muck had also worked its way into her hair and across the left side of her face—which had been plastered to the side of the small beast.

Molly Jacobs, who was covering the fund-raiser for her national newspaper column, suddenly jumped in front of her and snapped off a round of shots. Blinded by the rapid-fire flashes, Ashby blinked. What a mug shot that was going to be!

But it was over. That was all she could think as she stumbled toward the other women in the center of the arena.

"Way to go, Ashby." Lacy laughed. "You almost had him!"

Ashby thought it was the other way around. That pig had outwitted ten women. It was some pig.

Despite getting duped, the group clasped hands and lifted them up in triumph. To her dismay, they all seemed to have had a great time.

Ashby stank. They all did, but she was pretty sure she was the worst. She managed a semblance of a smile for the clapping audience, and reminded herself why she'd done this—this horrid, horrid thing. Perhaps it had not been in vain—it could even mark a turning point in her love life.

All she knew was that if this hadn't changed her image, nothing would.

Dan snaked through the crowd toward where the ladies were exiting the arena. That had been the funniest thing he'd seen in years. Watching nine ladies pile up on the piglet like a football team after a pigskin had been pretty entertaining. But when that squealing animal popped out of the pileup and headed for Ash, she'd looked like a little girl confronting the monster beneath her bed. Her eyes had grown to the size of plates and she'd gone as white as the pristine wedding dress hanging in her store window.

The woman was a real dynamo. Who'd ever have believed it! When she'd dived, despite her obvious apprehension, every cowboy around him had hollered and cheered. Dan had a feeling she'd accomplished her mission. He was proud of and relieved for her at the same time.

And he was off the hook…

Despite the tensions between them, he was compelled to speak to her. To let her know he thought she'd done well—even though he didn't think she'd care what he thought. He made it to the end of the stairs and was waiting a few feet from the exit as the ladies filed out. Ashby was at the tail end of the line. Her face was smudged with stuff he was quite certain she was trying hard not to think about. But her eyes were sparkling. Dan liked that.

Several of the single gals flirted with him on their way past. Beth Clark stopped to talk. She was excited and laughing, and he couldn't help but smile back at her. She was a pretty woman, though some would say her chin was too strong. Dan was looking at the life in her eyes. He'd seen her at the shelter, helping out a few times when he was there, so he knew she had a good heart. She was going to make some cowboy a lucky man one of these days.

Beth was still talking when Ashby came through the gate. Not wanting to be rude, he placed a hand on Beth's arm, halting her words momentarily with his touch.

"So how'd that feel?" he asked Ashby. She paused, her eyes meeting his, then flicking to Beth and back again.

"It was interesting."

The surprise in her voice made him grin. "Told you it would feel good to loosen up."

She tensed at his words and her eyes darkened. "Yes, you were right," she said, then turned and walked away.

Chapter Four

"Hey, Ash, wait up, would you?" Having finally gotten through the crowd, Dan reached her just as she opened her car door. She was looking at the interior with a perplexed expression, as if it had just dawned on her that she had a problem. Knowing her the way he thought he did, Dan figured she probably hadn't realized the state she'd be in coming out of that arena. Not that everyone had suffered the misfortune that she'd had, landing in that specific patch of dirt.

"What do you want?" She shot him a glare.

"Hold on to your bonnet. I didn't mean anything by what I said back there. I come in peace."

Her expression remained tense, but the hostility in her eyes eased as her gaze shifted from him to the inside of her T-Bird.

"How about I give you a ride into town? You can get cleaned up and come back for your car later tonight."

Her look turned skeptical. "Or tomorrow," he amended. "You can get someone else to swing you by."

She sucked in a deep breath. "I'll mess up your truck."

"Naw, you can ride in the truck bed." When alarm flared in her eyes, he chuckled. "Just kidding. My truck's built to handle the worst and keep on going. I'll just take a hose to the floorboards and some soap and water to the seat."

She stared at her car again. Dan took in the plush carpet lining the floor and the sporty bucket seats that were half cloth and half leather. "Those cow patties you rolled in aren't going to come out of that cloth anytime soon. If ever."

"I know. I'm a mess."

It suddenly hit him that she sounded depressed. He'd first thought it was because she was less than happy at seeing him, but now he wasn't so sure. He looked closer. "Are you okay?"

Her lip trembled. "I smell like an *outhouse.* I don't know *what* is in my hair and—" She clammed up suddenly but her lip still trembled.

That did it. Dan reached around her and picked her purse up off the seat. "Come on. Let's get you home."

She didn't move, just stared at him. He held in a frustrated breath. "Look, I know you don't have a stellar opinion of me, but unless you have a better offer, I'd suggest you take me up on this one." Well, that was a low blow. But she was being obstinate again. Just as she'd been the day of the bike race. Without waiting for her, he closed and locked her door and headed across the parking lot toward his truck.

When he reached it, he set her purse inside on the console and waited as she approached, almost dragging her feet. She really was a mess. It was going to take a gallon of heavy-duty cleaner to restore his truck after he dropped her off at her apartment. Still silent, she eased into the seat with a squish. She closed her eyes as the scent filled the interior of his truck.

"If they'd warned me about what was mixed in with the dirt after a rodeo, I would never have done this."

Dan chuckled, pulled the seat belt out and reached across her to buckle her in. She looked a little too shaken to manage it herself. The smell was worsening. He patted her knee before he closed the door. "Tomorrow you'll be glad you did it."

He was smiling as he hurried around to his side of the truck. She might be as prickly as a porcupine, but she sure had been something tackling that pig.

And he knew he wasn't the only cowboy who'd noticed.

Ashby had never been so relieved to see the big Victorian where she rented a small apartment come into view. Dan's kindness in the face of her dilemma had surprised her. She guessed she really was too much of a city girl to have realized she would be such a mess when the pig scramble was concluded.

Somehow, most of the others hadn't seemed to be in such a hideous state. Just her luck.

Dan whistled as he drove her into town, but didn't try to talk, almost as if he knew she needed time to wind down.

"Here you go," he said, pulling into the driveway. "Anything else I can do for you?"

What did he mean by that?

"Don't look so horrified. I only wanted to know if you needed me to hose you down in the backyard, or help you pull off those boots." He grinned, and in the light of the dash, she could see his eyes twinkling.

"Thank you, but I'm fine." Ashby climbed stiffly out of the truck and gasped when she looked back at the seat.

"Don't worry, I'll get this cleaned up the minute I get home."

That was the most optimistic thing Ashby had heard all day. She nodded. "Well, thanks again for the ride. Good night." The mortification of the entire evening was rapidly collapsing in on her. She closed the door and hurried toward the apartment house. She'd just stepped onto the sidewalk when Dan called her name. She turned to find him watching her through the open window.

"Sweet dreams, Ash. You did good." He tipped his hat, then drove off.

She watched his taillights until they disappeared, reminding herself that the man had charming women down to a science. She could not let a nice gesture and a couple of kind words get to her.

Dan was trouble. He couldn't be trusted. Men like him could appear sincere when it suited them. With a simple smile they could draw women like the proverbial moth to flame. Steven's charm had worked the same way. She had believed every word of his lies until she'd found him kissing his secretary. Yes, charm was shallow. Men like Steven couldn't be trusted and she'd do well to remember that every time Dan opened his mouth.

Easier said than done, Ashby thought the next morning as she looked up from her sweeping to see Dan sauntering down the sidewalk toward her. He was smiling that slow, easy smile of his, and though she'd been avoiding meetings like this for the past month, etiquette required her to stand her ground today, given his courtesy the previous night.

"Mornin', Ash," he drawled, coming to a halt a few steps away from her. "Letting your hair down agrees with you. You're looking as pretty as an apple blossom this morning."

Ashby's pulse skipped. This wasn't a personal observation, it was just Dan. He'd been at the candy store and he had probably spent thirty minutes flirting with all the ladies who worked there. It was a usual stop for him, but he didn't have her fooled—no one ate that much candy.

"Good morning," she said, her hands tightening on the broom. Her resistance was irrational today and she knew it. The man had given her a ride home when, frankly, no one else had come near her—with good reason! She'd almost cried when she'd seen herself in her bathroom mirror last night. "I hope your truck is okay today." She had awakened feeling totally embarrassed about the entire evening before.

"It's good. Told you it would be." He leaned forward and inhaled deeply. "You smell much better today."

Ashby felt her cheeks warm. From embarrassment, plain and simple.

He grinned and wiggled the bag in front of her. "Would you like a piece of candy?"

Okay, so maybe he really did have a sweet tooth, and he wasn't just over there flirting. The ladies from the women's shelter, who ran the store, did make some of the best confections she'd ever tasted. And it wasn't her business, anyway, what this man did and didn't do.

"No, thank you," she managed to reply. "I wanted to thank you once more for your help last night." She resumed sweeping, hoping he would pass on by.

He nibbled a chocolate peanut cluster and continued to study her. "Got any dates lined up yet?"

"No," she snapped. Humiliation spurred her to sweep faster. A moment passed, and then he bent his knees and playfully peeked up at her, with irritatingly happy eyes. "You're mad about last night, aren't you?"

Ashby scowled at him and kept working.

"C'mon, Ash. You don't have anything to be ashamed about. You gave it your best shot and you proved me wrong. And you clean up nice—did I already say that?"

Knowing that he actually knew why she'd scrambled

for the pig was the problem. She couldn't tell if the burn she felt was from sunshine or embarrassment.

Well, he could just go away. Nothing would suit her more. As a matter of fact, *all* the rotten men of Mule Hollow could keep their distance. She didn't need any of them. For the moment, she was so upset that sounded exactly right. Gave her some semblance of satisfaction.

And still Dan lingered.

"I'm on my way over to Sam's to grab a cup of coffee and catch up on the morning news. Join me? We can have an early lunch."

Did the man never give up? "I'm working." She inhaled slowly, calmly. "But thank you, anyway," she added, looking up at him as she struggled to hang on to her manners. She was five-eight—five-eleven in the three-inch heels she wore—and still she had to look up at him. Her lips curved in a tight smile of dismissal.

To her dismay, he leaned against the doorjamb and crossed his booted feet. His spurs sang, drawing her gaze. It was apparent that even though it was ten in the morning, Dan had already been working. There was a fine layer of dust covering the lower edges of his sun-faded jeans, and traces of red mud on his boots. The man might move with a slow grace that made him seem lazy, but Ashby knew he was a hard worker, splitting his time between his horse-shoeing business, his cattle-buying operation and running his own herd. That was the reason he could eat all that candy and not have it show up on his waist.

"Ash, didn't your mamma teach you it's not nice to stare?" he drawled.

"I wasn't staring. Your spurs distracted me." Amazing, just amazing, how easy it was to let her guard slip around him. And he knew it, too. Her eyes narrowed as she met his smug expression head-on.

Not affected in the least by her ire, he nodded toward the interior of her store. "I couldn't help noticing that you don't have any customers, Miss Templeton," he teased. "If a man didn't know any better, he'd think you didn't want to be seen with him. It's just lunch, Ash. Or coffee. Take your pick. I'm easy."

"No, thank you," she said, fighting to remain aloof. She'd been doing so for a year now and the man's persistence was amazing. She was probably the only woman on the planet who had ever turned him down—thus she understood she represented a challenge. He might even feel sorry for her. That stung. She held his gaze, refusing to give in to the dark emotions.

He bit into the peanut cluster and mimicked her aloof expression. "Sure you don't want one of these? You know, the ladies next door do know how to make chocolate."

Ashby shook her head, while her mouth watered.

For the candy.

"Don't tell me you're on a diet." He regarded her skeptically.

"That, cowboy, wouldn't be any of your business."

He chuckled and his eyes sparked. "That's not my

fault. It's not like I haven't been trying to get to know you better."

And that was all the reminder she needed to get her head on straight. "That, in a nutshell, is why I'd never go out with you. You are incorrigible, *Mr. Dawson.*"

He beamed! "Well, thank ya, darlin'. I was wondering when you were going to notice."

"It wasn't a compliment," she said dryly. "You try to 'get to know' every woman within driving distance."

"Oh, now you're wounding me." He covered his heart with the bag of candy.

She'd heard him make that statement many times and end it with his hand over his heart. Personally, Ashby felt it was a bit clichéd. Still, it made her own heart skip a beat. "We both know that's impossible," she snapped.

He startled her when he pushed away from the building to step close to her. "Maybe you don't know me as well as you think you do, Ash."

Unnerved by his proximity, she reached for the door. "I'll take your word for it. Enjoy your coffee."

He reached for the door, too, and his hand covered hers. Their eyes locked and held as every fiber of her being sizzled to life. She couldn't move, and she hated herself for it.

He tugged on the handle, his smile blooming. "Don't look so shocked, Ash. My mom taught me to open doors for ladies."

When she noticed the twinkle in his eyes was verging

on mirth, her good sense started making a comeback. This man knew the effect he had on her. He knew the effect he had on *all* women.

She yanked her hand back. Anger flashed through her that she'd reacted in such a pedestrian manner. "Thank you, but I could have done it myself." She started to step past him. His hand on her arm stopped her.

"Like I said before, you need to loosen up, Ash." His voice softened. "Is that why you're afraid of me?"

Afraid? She lifted her chin. "I'm not afraid of you. You are just not what I'm looking for in a man."

His eyes said he didn't believe her. The way her pulse was going haywire, she wasn't so sure she believed herself. But she knew what was good for her and what wasn't.

"Ash, I think we both know you're not being honest. Go out with me." His voice grew husky. "Or at least have lunch with me. What could it hurt?"

Ashby's resolve faltered. She stiffened her back and squared her jaw. "My name is Ashby and I'm not interested in having lunch with a playboy." It sounded ugly, but it was as much for her own ears as for his.

His jaw tensed, but surprisingly he said nothing as she strode past him across the threshold, all too aware that he was watching her. All too mad at herself for losing control. The door closed with a refined click, as if to chide her.

The man took nothing seriously.

And she would do well to remember that bit of important information. She was looking for a husband. God's man for her. Dan Dawson…

She watched him saunter toward Sam's Diner, then turned her back to the window, putting the carefree flirtation out of her thoughts. Dan wasn't that kind of man.

Not when she knew he'd probably stopped thinking about her the moment he'd stepped off the sidewalk and walked away.

Chapter Five

"Morning, Applegate and Stanley," Dan said as he entered Sam's Diner. It was midmorning, so the only customers were the two old-timers huddled over their perpetual game of checkers.

"So, did she turn ya down agin?" Applegate almost shouted, his wrinkled frown lifting into a craggy grin.

Dan slid onto a worn buckskin stool. "You know she did."

The two old men stared at him.

Last night after dropping her off at her place, Dan vowed to back off, yet one look at her this morning and there he went.… "I guess either I'm a glutton for punishment, or I just like needling her." He pushed his hat off his forehead. "What do you boys think?"

Sam came out from the kitchen, a small, wiry man with a brisk walk. Lifting the pot of coffee, he filled a cup for Dan without even asking. "It's both," he said as he poured. "I gotta warn ya, though, you better be watching yor back."

"Look, fellas," Dan said, not at all concerned with Sam's unvoiced fears. "I'm well aware that the matchmakers have their eyes on me. Why do you think that is?" They'd seemed happy to leave him alone all this time.

"Why?" Stanley's jovial expression changed to a smirk. "'Cause now that they've got the hang of this matchmaking, it's like they can't stop."

Applegate nodded solemnly. "It is kinda enjoyable. I done got into it myself. But I ain't so sure they're gonna have thar way with Dan here."

Sam slapped the towel he'd been wiping the counter with over his shoulder. "I told my Adela that very thang. I told her Dan was a born bachelor if ever thar was one."

Dan nursed his coffee and listened to the boys. He probably did look like a born bachelor to them, and he was, to an extent. But he planned to get married someday. He wasn't sure about having children…but marriage was something he hoped for, when the time was right. Despite what most people saw on the outside, he was a very cautious man. Marriage wasn't something to rush. He was only twenty-eight and had a lot to accomplish before taking on that kind of responsibility. When he offered his name to a lady, there would be nothing more serious in all of his life. Though for the time being, the matchmaking ladies of Mule Hollow would have to be content fixing up others.

He wouldn't hold it against the ladies for trying. They would realize the futility of their efforts soon enough. In the meantime, he didn't mind in the least being their entertainment.

Of course, he didn't think Ashby felt the same way.

Dan took a swig of coffee, savoring the flavor. Life needed to be savored, every moment enjoyed and celebrated. Ash needed to learn that, which was why he teased her so much.

Although it rankled him just a bit that she continued to refuse to go out with him. He had to admit that she'd tried his patience more than he'd thought possible. Like refusing to ride the bike. He was still baffled about that. Even if her friends had set her up, she should have been cooperative.

Her recent efforts in the pig scramble had impressed him. He grinned, thinking about the way she'd stood out from the crowd last night.

"You sure do have a smile on yor face about something," Sam said, breaking into his thoughts.

Dan set the cup down. "I was just thinking about that pig scramble last night."

Sam's face crinkled. "I never figured such a prim and proper lady like Ashby ta get out thar with a pig. Wonder what made her decide ta do that?"

Dan kept his lips sealed, steering the conversation on to other things as he ate his lunch.

"Well, fellas," he said when he was done, "it's been nice talking to you, but I've got a load of cattle waiting patiently on me to haul them to San Antonio." He headed toward the door.

"Didn't you carry a load up there last week?" Applegate asked, halting his red checker in midair.

"That was a load to the ranch this side of Georgetown, not that far."

"You sure been keeping busy," Stanley said, scowling when Applegate removed one of his checkers.

"There isn't any other way to be, is there?" Dan said. "See y'all later."

Leaving the diner, he headed for his truck and trailer parked in the vacant lot at the end of Main Street. He could hear the cattle bawling as he approached. It was a nice load that would earn him a tidy profit. Always a good thing. His small ranch was almost paid for, and if he kept up the pace of his earnings, it'd be all his before the year was out. Part of that came from having no responsibilities to anyone but himself and the good Lord. Being single had its advantages.

Climbing into the truck, he started it up and glanced toward Ashby's shop. She didn't think much of him. As he drove away, he knew that particular failure bothered him more than he wanted to admit. And he wasn't sure why.

Turning off Main Street, he headed toward the crossroads that would take him the fifty miles to the highway. He couldn't help thinking about the way she'd looked the night before, sitting on the ground in the middle of that arena.

Dazed, confused and totally out of her element.

He should have felt guilty for having goaded her into taking on the pig scramble, but he didn't. It was for her own good, beyond trying to make those dimwitted cowboys take notice of her.

All the other gals who'd been in that arena had had a ball letting their hair down for a good cause. Ashby Templeton had just been there for the good cause.

Sad thing was she didn't even know there was a difference.

Ashby loved Sunday mornings. She always made it a point to go by the nursery and hold all the little ones before she went into Sunday school. The ladies took turns in the nursery on a rotating basis. Her morning or not, Ashby went by to say hello to the toddlers. Up until a few months ago, Mule Hollow had only had a one-year-old baby boy to fill the church nursery. But when Dottie and Brady Cannon had opened the women's shelter, the nursery was blessed with the addition of a darling set of three-year-old twins and a fifteen-month-old toddler. The more the merrier, Ashby thought, and she fully expected that with all the weddings that had been happening around town recently, there were bound to be more soon.

Oh, that she could be one of those parents.

Rose, who worked part-time at the dress store for Ashby and was also a resident of the women's shelter, waved her inside. "I've been expecting you."

Smiling, she handed over fifteen-month-old Bryce. His mother, Stacy, had come to the shelter with Rose when it relocated to Mule Hollow. Abused by her father and later the man she'd married to escape him, Stacy was very fragile. She'd only found the courage to escape from the abuse after she'd given birth to her beautiful baby boy, and had had a chance encounter with Rose. A God-given encounter that led Rose to tell her about a way out of the abuse. Rose and Ashby had become good friends over the past few months, and Ashby had great respect for her.

Looking into the eyes of this child, and knowing that he was going to grow up in such a loving community, Ashby felt her heart rejoice.

"I was running late," she said. "But you know I had to come by and see my favorite people in all the world." She tickled Bryce in the tummy and he rewarded her with a cackling laugh. He was a darling with dark hair, sleepy eyes and a smile that sent shafts of sunshine to her heart.

"That's okay. Saying hello to these babies is just as important as getting to class on time. You're their favorite babysitter, after all. When you come out to the shelter and watch the boys while we go to workshops or counseling sessions, their moms rest easy. It's a great blessing."

"I love helping out, babysitting these fellas especially," she said, as two sets of tiny arms hugged her knees. "How are my little men?" She stooped to accept hugs from the three-year-old twins.

Rose laughed. "You need some of your own."

Ashby sighed, looking up from her little group. Unwittingly, Rose had voiced Ashby's heart's desire.

"Tell me about it. I'm so ready, but I'm afraid I might have to admit defeat before long."

The boys had spied the animal crackers Rose was setting out, and were now intent on getting to chairs at the table. Ashby cuddled Bryce as Rose bent to say a brief prayer over the snack. It was a touching scene. Ashby joined Rose's prayers silently, giving the Lord thanks for the children's safety.

"I guess that means you didn't get any invitations to dinner from participating in the pig scramble?" Rose asked.

"Well," she hedged, "almost two days and no calls but…I did get one for lunch yesterday."

"Let me guess. Dan."

She nodded. "Not that I count it as a real invitation. The man asks everyone out. He's probably already taken every new face in town out to dinner."

"Are you jealous?" Rose asked.

"Don't be ridiculous. Why would you suggest such a thing?"

"Ashby, everyone can see the way the two of you spark off each other like flint rocks."

"It's a common phenomenon with him." She gave Bryce one last kiss on the head and handed him over, missing having him in her arms immediately. "I mean, really, don't you feel electricity when the man enters a room? He's just like that."

Rose's dark eyes flared. "Actually, no. The guy is good-looking, but he's not my type. That doesn't seem to be your opinion."

"Yes, it is. He and I are such opposites we make a complete circle on the compatibility chart."

Rose frowned. "Isn't that a good thing? That's how two people complement each other. You know, like the colors of a color wheel."

"Hate to say it, but I don't put much stock in all that kind of stuff. Trust me. The man and I do not match."

Rose smiled. "You might not match, but you sure do make for good entertainment."

Not certain what to say to that, Ashby just waved goodbye as she headed down the hall toward the singles class. Pausing outside the door, she smoothed her ice-blue silk skirt and straightened her necklace where Bryce had twisted it with his chubby little hand. The sweet baby loved all things that glittered. She'd learned from experience not to wear dangling earrings to the nursery.

As she opened the door and stepped inside, all eyes turned toward her. Her heart sank when she saw that there was only one empty chair in the room. Next to Dan.

He patted the chair. "Miss Templeton, I saved a seat just for you, darlin'."

Her eyes narrowed. "Thank you so much, *Mr. Dawson.* And to think I was afraid I'd have to stand in the corner for being late." She was all too aware of the smiles that ricocheted around the room. Lance Yates was sitting at the back, and she wondered why a nice man like him couldn't have saved her a chair. He was the kind of man she could fall in love with. Nice and steady.

Grudgingly, she took the seat, almost jumping when Dan leaned toward her.

"Not a chance of that happening on my watch. My mamma taught me to always let a lady have my chair." His breath tickled the sensitive skin of her neck, effectively ruining her chance at a convincing comeback.

Sheriff Brady drew the class back to where he'd been when she'd interrupted. He was a stickler for detail and preparation, always well-equipped with insightful takes on the scripture. He was a born teacher. And the men respected him. Because of him, more and more cowboys were starting to turn up on Sunday mornings. Of course, rumor had it he was changing some community service fines into Sunday school time. It was the only explanation for a few of the rougher cowboys showing up at irregular intervals.

Ashby had wondered if that was why Dan came each week. But even she didn't really believe that. There was absolutely nothing childlike about his familiarity with God's word. Knowledge such as he possessed came from time spent reading and studying scripture.

It made her feel a little guilty that she'd called him a playboy the day before. That niggled at her all through class as she listened to his participation in the discussions. To her dismay, she found herself feeling convicted that she needed to clarify her statement of the day before. Maybe other instances, too. She was taking frustrations out on Dan that weren't completely his fault. He was a flirt and he got under her skin on a regular basis, but the real issue was larger than that. He symbolized everything she wasn't looking for.

She made excuses all through class as to why she didn't need to apologize, but the conviction that she should wouldn't ease up. It must be done.

When class was over, Brady asked Dan to hang back to discuss a work-related problem. Something about horseshoes and hay. Ashby was relieved, because it gave everyone else time to head over to the sanctuary for the main service. She'd agreed she needed to make amends to Dan, but the whole world didn't need to hear it. She waited patiently in the hall as everyone filed past her.

"Hello, Ashby," Lance said, halting beside her. "Nice day."

"Yes, it is," she said, looking up at him. He really was a good-looking man, with his sandy-blond hair and brown eyes. Out of the blue she found herself comparing his mild eyes with Dan's intense ones. She pushed those startling thoughts away and smiled at him. "Brady taught a nice lesson, didn't he?"

"I enjoy the class." Lance cleared his throat and tapped his hat against his thigh. "You did a good job with that pig the other night." His eyes lit up a bit as he delivered the compliment. Ashby brightened. Maybe he was going to ask her out.

"Dan got you home okay?"

She nodded. "Thank goodness. I was in terrible shape. He came to my rescue." Now why did she say that?

Lance looked mildly uncomfortable. "Well, I just wanted to say hello. I'll see you later."

A little perplexed by the awkward exchange, Ashby watched him walk away. At least she was able to talk to the man without feeling as if she were standing on the deck of a ship in an electrical storm, which was how she felt with Dan.

What was keeping him? Whatever the two men were discussing dragged on, and she began losing her nerve. Maybe she should do this elsewhere.

She was about to leave when the two men strode out of the classroom.

"Hey, Ashby," Brady said. "Did you need me for something? Sorry about that. Dan's helping me out in the morning and we got carried away talking plans."

"Oh, that's okay." She met Dan's gaze and that aggravating electricity surged around them. Especially when he winked at her. "Actually, I needed to speak to Dan." She wanted to disappear beneath the welcome mat when Brady's knowing smile widened.

"Well, well," he said. "Why didn't you say so? Glad to have both of you in class this morning."

Dan's grin mirrored Brady's and he leaned against the wall expectantly. Did he not know how to stand up straight?

The minute the other man left them, Ashby whirled

toward Dan, apology forgotten. "What is wrong with you?"

"Me? You said you wanted to see me. What'd I do?"

Narrowing her eyes, she slammed her hands on her hips. "The winking, the flirting. The grinning. It's like a woman can't have a decent conversation with you because you go mucking it up with your—with your obnoxious, condescending behavior."

Why couldn't *some* men grow up?

He studied her for a long moment as she fought to rein in her uncharacteristic flare of temper. "What are you afraid of?" he asked, his voice going mellow, his gaze penetrating all the way into her soul.

She wished he'd stop asking her that question. It always put her off balance. "Nothing," she snapped, moving away from him.

"Ash, what is the harm in flirting? There certainly isn't anything in it meant to be insulting."

She fumbled for a plausible reason for her temper tantrum. Steven's betrayal came to mind, but really, Dan meant nothing to her, so why did she let him get to her so? "There's a time and a place for it, and church isn't the place."

He crossed his arms and cocked his head to the side, studying her. "You're right. I'm sorry."

Primed to detail the inappropriateness of the situation, she was disarmed by his acquiescence.

He leaned toward her. "Normally, when someone apologizes, the injured party says something. You know—'Thank you, kind sir, for the quick and heartfelt apology.' Something of that nature." He lifted a perfect eyebrow, thick and straight. "C'mon, try it."

So much for acquiescence. She gave up, shook her head and marched down the sidewalk toward the front of the church. There was just no seriousness to the man at all. He was incorrigible. She'd said it once and she was saying it again. And to think she'd tried to apologize to him!

Chapter Six

Dan watched Ashby stalk away, and felt the sting of guilt for having taken it too far. He caught up with her at the door. "Ash, wait. I'm sorry. Really. I'm not normally so—"

She pinned him with fierce eyes, and he blanked out the rest of the sentence. They were standing on the porch. The doors were already closed and he could hear Miss Adela's piano playing signal to everyone it was time to take their seats.

"Not normally so what? Rude, overbearing, full of yourself?"

His jaw tensed. "Well, that's a bit harsh even for you, Ash."

She looked off into the distance briefly, then back at him with slightly contrite eyes.

"Maybe I overreacted." She sounded as if she

couldn't really believe that's what might have happened. "But are you ever serious about anything?"

"Only if I have to be." He grinned, hoping to lighten things up, but she didn't appreciate his joke at all. Nope, she turned pinker than she already was.

"Do you think that women don't have enough brains in their heads to carry on a conversation that doesn't start with a wink, a joke or pick-up line?" she asked. "Well, we can, you know." She yanked open the door and stalked into the packed house.

Stunned by the dressing-down, Dan stood in the doorway, watching her stomp up the center aisle. She took a seat in a crowded pew, making everyone shift like a flank of dominos.

"Maybe you overreacted a whole bunch," he mumbled, and stepped inside. He took an empty seat in the back row beside Applegate Thornton.

The older man grinned. "She turn ya down agin?" he asked, loudly enough for everyone within four rows to hear.

Dan felt eyes glancing his way. "Something like that," he grumbled, and picked up a hymnal.

He *talked* to women. He didn't flirt all the time. Besides, flirting usually made women smile.

Stubborn female. He'd come to church to worship the Lord, but as the service got started he was having a hard time getting his mind off the hardheaded woman six rows up. She acted like he'd brought down the entire women's movement with a simple wink! She'd really rubbed him the wrong way with her accusations.

He was lost in thought, really getting wound up when, suddenly, Brady stood up and hurried out of his pew. In his hand, he held the emergency beeper that he wore on his belt, and as he walked out the door he had Dan's full attention.

Because of the small size of Mule Hollow, Brady was not only the sheriff, but the main contact for all emergency situations. Everyone pitched in when there was a need, and as Brady disappeared, Dan kept one eye on the door, knowing he'd come back and recruit help if the situation called for it.

Though he'd slipped out quietly, the whole congregation was distracted from the song they were singing by the realization of what his departure meant. A small-town emergency could be anything from a cow stuck in a tank to an eighteen-wheeler turned over at the crossroads. Fires and illnesses topped the list of things that could happen.

Almost as soon as Brady walked out the door, he was back. Grim-faced, he strode inside, meeting Dan's gaze straight on.

A feeling of foreboding rippled through Dan as he stepped out of the pew and walked forward. "What is it, Brady?"

The music came to a complete halt, and everyone in the small sanctuary went silent.

"It's your place, Dan. It's on fire."

* * *

It was pretty useless to try to keep a small town away from a fire, so Sheriff Brady didn't try. Ashby watched as Dan took off for his truck. Clint Matlock, Bob Jacobs and the other men who made up the Mule Hollow volunteer fire department were right behind him as they raced back to town to grab their gear and Mule Hollow's one and only fire truck. It was an older model loaded with a large water tank. In the country, fire hydrants weren't around to connect to, and when the water ran out, a fire won.

Ashby knew as well as anyone that if the blaze had been burning long, the situation was grim. With the time it took to get to the truck, then out to Dan's place, the crew had little likelihood of saving whatever was on fire. The most they could hope was to stop it from becoming a hazard to surrounding homes and livestock.

Prayer flowed ceaselessly from Ashby's lips as she followed the procession the eight miles to Dan's. She was less than thrilled with the man, but she hated that this was happening to him.

It was plain to see by the heavy dark smoke billowing into the blue sky that the fire was big. Ashby prayed harder as the miles flew by—that God would protect Dan's animals and those who were going to be fighting the flames, Dan in particular.

Guilt assailed her. She might have been a bit rough on him earlier, but she knew that if Dan's barn was on fire and there were any animals in danger, he would rush into the flames to save them.

Ahead of them, Brady turned into Dan's drive. Seconds later, Ashby and the caravan from church careened over the cattle guard, turning into the pasture off the lane. They had to leave the gravel driveway open so that the fire truck would have access.

Ashby's heart sank as she clambered out of her car. Black smoke billowed from Dan's home and flames were starting to break through the roof in several places. Everyone ran across the grass, hoping to be of help in any way possible. The men were shouting instructions, and the women, Norma Sue and Esther Mae in particular, were passing them on in a chain. Ashby heard everything going on around her as if from a distance, like the static of several radio stations fighting to be heard. Her attention was focused ahead of her, on Dan's home and the smoke rolling out of the open front door.

Struggling to catch her breath, she felt her heart pound in her ears as she stumbled to a halt near the back of Sheriff Brady's truck. She scanned the area, coughing. Where was Dan?

Nowhere in sight. Her eyes locked on the open door and she felt as if she was going to be sick. The house was burning with terrifying intensity. Was Dan inside?

With a sinking heart, she realized Brady must think so, because he was strapping on his oxygen tank as he headed toward the doorway.

Ashby couldn't believe what was happening. The fire truck could be heard approaching. *Hurry,* she prayed over and over. As she watched, a section of roof caved in, and she screamed. Burning ash and debris scattered, catching the dry grass on fire everywhere it landed. She knew as well as anyone the danger if the sparks were left unattended. But all she could think about was that somewhere inside the flaming house, Dan had disappeared. And Brady was going in after him.

Like worker ants, people raced to dowse the flames licking across the yard before they could get out of hand. But Ashby couldn't pull herself away from where she stood, crazy with fear. The fire truck finally rumbled across the cattle guard, and she felt some relief, knowing it was here. But it was too late for the house.

Suddenly, before Brady could make it inside, Dan staggered out the door, barely visible in the black smoke. Brady grabbed him just as he was collapsing. And that's when Ashby moved, knowing they were still in danger. First she grabbed the picture frame Dan was clutching, then she scooted beneath his arm and helped Brady get him to clean air.

He was coughing so hard she thought he would break in two as they reached the truck. Brady yanked the tailgate down, told him to sit, and gave him oxygen.

"Watch him, Ashby. And don't let him do any more stupid stunts. The ambulance is on its way."

Ashby nodded, meeting Dan's red eyes over the rim of the oxygen mask. To her surprise, he winked!

Brady squeezed her shoulder. "There's bottled water in the pickup. Would you get him some? And call me if you need me."

Ashby nodded again and went for the water as Brady hurried off. She snatched a bottle out of the twenty-four pack in Brady's back seat. Obviously, he stayed prepared for trouble.

Dan was still coughing as she set the picture on the tailgate beside him. He took the water from her, and after a few swallows his coughs eased a little.

"Had to get—"

"Don't talk," Ashby said, gently pushing the hand holding the oxygen mask back up to his face. He watched her as he took a breath.

Foolish man. She glanced at the picture. It was of him several years younger, and a woman who looked enough like him that it had to be his mother. Ashby felt the prick of tears. He'd risked his life for a picture of his mother. Her heart melted.

She met his gaze. Behind the mask she could perceive a faint smile. "Your mother?" she asked, though she knew the answer.

He nodded. "Important," he wheezed between coughs. "She died."

Ashby looked toward the house as emotion took over and tears slid down her cheeks. He'd gone into a raging fire to save a photo of his dead mother.

She wanted to tell him it was stupid to have risked his life for a picture. But she couldn't.

The ambulance pulled into the yard and she swiped the dampness off her cheeks, catching him watching her as she waved the emergency vehicle over.

He touched her arm. “Don’t cry,” he said, his voice hoarse. “Just stuff.” His eyes, red from the smoke, held her gaze. He’d just lost everything and *he* was comforting *her.* Before she could react, the EMTs were there, telling her to step aside.

She did, though she hovered close. For the first time since she’d known Dan Dawson, she let herself admit her curiosity about him.

And so that was that, Dan thought, standing near the heap of ashes that had been his home up until four hours ago. Parts of the house remained standing, charred and smoldering. The roof was caved in, and what was left inside…if the fire hadn’t destroyed it, the water had. It was almost easier to look at the ashes than at the smutty residue that fire and water left on the few things that remained: pots and pans, framed pictures, the images behind the glass spoiled by the smoke and water that had seeped through the edges.

He thanked the Lord for giving him time to save the picture of him and his mom. That was all he had left of her now. If he’d arrived five minutes later, he wouldn’t have been able to make the mad dash into the house to snatch the framed eight-by-ten off the wall in the den.

Brady hadn’t given him a dressing-down for the stunt, and Dan was sure the only reason was that he knew it wouldn’t have done any good. The sheriff had tried to get him to go to the hospital, but Dan had refused. That hadn’t made the EMTs or Ashby happy.

He thought of the tears he'd seen in her eyes, and his chest grew tighter than it already was. Her tender heart had touched him.

The growing mental list of what needed to be done quickly pushed his thoughts away from Ashby. But until the adjuster came out there wasn't much he could actually do. First thing tomorrow, he intended to have copies of the photo made, and to put one in a safe-deposit box. His mother had been a special lady, and the thought of not being able to show his some-day children a picture of their grandmother was unbearable.

He'd never known a stronger woman than his mother. She'd risked everything for him, her only child, even her life.... Her grandchildren would need to see a picture of her, and thanks to the Lord's timing, they would...that is, *if* he ever had any.

"Man, I'm really sorry," Clint said, coming to stand beside him. "This is a cryin' shame. Did I hear Brady tell you it was a faulty lamp cord?"

"Can you believe it? Plugged into the outlet beside my bed." Dan met his friend's sympathetic eyes and pulled a smile up despite the situation. "At least no one was hurt."

"Well, there is that. Though you took a big risk. You feeling okay?"

Dan nodded.

"I wish there had been more we could do," Clint added.

Dan knew he was in shock to an extent, and that tomorrow he might feel differently, but... "It's just stuff, Clint. I've never been big on creature comforts, anyway."

"Yeah, well, I agree with you on that." He glanced toward Lacy, who was chatting with a group of women. "As long as I walked out of something like this with Lacy alive, that's all that would matter to me."

Dan nodded. "You've got your priorities straight."

"Look, I was serious about coming to stay at the house for as long as you need to."

Dan had received so many offers they were all a blur, but this time he accepted. "Thanks, buddy, I'll take you up on it tonight. I'll figure something else out tomorrow. Now, help me get everyone to go on home. I know they all want to pitch in but there's nothing anyone can do now."

It took them a little while to get the townsfolk to listen, but eventually they all walked back out to their cars and headed home for the evening. Dan got hugs from all the women and plenty of back slaps from the guys. They were good people.

He watched everyone leave, promising that he was going to go out to Clint's right after everyone left. But even though he loved them all dearly, he was glad to see them go. He needed a few moments alone.

Chapter Seven

"Are you sure you don't need me anymore?" Rose asked, excitement lacing her voice.

Ashby looked up from where she was working on her Web site.

"Yes, go. You have more important things to attend to today. It isn't every day that your son turns fourteen."

"Tell me about it! There isn't much more that needs to be done. Living in a house full of bakers and candy makers has its advantages."

Ashby could only imagine the treats Max and his friends were in for tonight. She laughed. Dottie oversaw the shelter, and taught the women the trade of candy making and baking, along with basic business skills. Her ministry was working out wonderfully for the ladies. And Mule Hollow.

"You're coming, right?" Rose pulled her purse from

beneath the counter beside where Ashby sat studying the computer screen.

"Seven o'clock. I'll be there."

Rose checked out the dress Ashby was considering. "Beautiful. Are you ordering that for the store or is it going to be exclusive to the Web site?"

"It's for the site, but I'm thinking I'll bring a couple in for us here."

Rose glanced around at the eclectic mix of fashionable merchandise Ashby had filled the store with.

"This place is amazing," she said.

Ashby smiled proudly. Because she'd started a successful Web site that catered to a wealthy clientele, she was able to mix a few of those items in with a wonderful variety of merchandise in a price range more accessible to the average shopper, many of whom Mule Hollow was now drawing on a regular basis.

Ashby delighted in traveling into the heart of Texas Hill Country seeking out talented people making unique items, the beaded denim jackets and hand-tooled leather belts that everyone loved, for example.

"You have a gift, Ashby. I never thought I'd be working in a place like this. Or that Max would be turning fourteen in such a wonderful environment as Mule Hollow."

Ashby hugged her. "The town is blessed to have you here. And I couldn't do without you. Now go or you'll be rushed."

"Right. See you there."

Ashby felt blessed herself as she watched Rose leave. There were never enough hours in the day to keep things fresh on her site and in the store. Rose helped immensely and enabled her to take a day off here and there.

Such as tomorrow afternoon, when she would go help with the cleanup at Dan's. Since the fire almost a week earlier, she hadn't seen much of him. But she'd thought of him. Actually, it was more than that. She couldn't *stop* thinking about him.

She'd told herself over and over that nothing had changed about him. He'd gone into his home to save a picture of his mother. It didn't alter the man as she knew him.

At five o'clock, she closed up and headed down the sidewalk to her apartment house. The lovely Victorian with white siding and green turrets added so much to Mule Hollow's ambience, sitting at the west end of Main Street. Ashby loved living there, though her neighbors had been changing on a regular basis lately. Of all the women who had originally rented apartments when she'd come, Ashby was now the only one who remained. The other single women had married and moved away. And the cycle began again with new occupants. The apartment across the hall from her had just become empty and she expected to see someone moving in any day.

She was passing Sam's Diner when she saw Adela, Norma Sue and Esther Mae sitting out front at the green picnic table. When they beckoned for her to join them, she detoured for a quick visit.

"Sit down and have a glass of lemonade with us," Esther Mae said.

Norma Sue patted the bright green bench beside her. Sinking onto it, Ashby accepted the glass Adela held out to her.

"You are coming out to Dan's tomorrow to help with the cleanup, aren't you?" Norma Sue asked.

"Yes. Rose is going to work the store for me."

"Good," Esther Mae said. "It's such a shame that he lost everything. Everything, that is, but his mamma's picture. That boy does love his mamma. Ashby, you do know that boys who love their mothers make good husbands."

Ashby hoped that was true, but she didn't know if that was a real statistic or an Esther Mae statistic. She realized, belatedly, that she should have kept on walking.

"We know you're not so sure about that when it comes to our boy Dan. But he's a good man," Norma Sue said.

She could admit that she had a newfound curiosity about him, but that didn't change the fact that he was no match for her. "Have any of you ever cleaned up after a fire?" she asked, hoping to change the subject.

Adela nodded. "Be certain not to wear anything you don't want ruined. That soot just refuses to come out."

"You know that boy hasn't stopped working." Norma Sue changed the topic midstream. "Lacy said he's been carrying on like nothing happened. Made a trip somewhere the day before yesterday for a load of cattle. Poor boy hasn't even got a bed to call his own, but he's working as hard as ever. And to think, all because of a good-for-nothing lamp cord. All I can say is the good Lord works in mysterious ways."

Adela smiled, meeting Norma Sue's sympathetic gaze. "Yes, He does, so don't fret."

Ashby was a bit baffled by what they meant by the Lord working in mysterious ways where Dan's fire was concerned, but she knew they wouldn't rest until they got him settled. Although she felt certain Clint and Lacy would want him to stay with them as long as he needed to. "Well, I enjoyed the company but I need to go home and change. I'm supposed to help out at Max's birthday party."

"I think that's great," Esther Mae exclaimed a little too exuberantly. Ashby looked at her curiously and the woman turned as crimson as her hair. "You know what I mean. It's good that Rose has a friend like you. And to think little Max is turning fourteen. Of course, you might need some help out there with all those rambunctious boys running around. I sure do hope there will be some men to lend a hand."

Norma Sue's and Adela's faces were suspiciously blank. Ashby reassessed Esther Mae's.

"Sheriff Brady will be there. I'm sure he can handle anything that the teenagers can throw his way." She stood. "I'd better go if I'm going to be on time. I'll see all of you tomorrow."

"Ashby, you have fun out there tonight," Norma Sue said, her mile-wide smile stretching mischievously across her round face.

Ashby said a quick goodbye, then crossed the street and headed straight for her apartment. Thinking about Norma Sue's smile, she couldn't help feeling as if she'd escaped something.

The house was quiet as she made her way up the steps leading to her apartment. What were the ladies planning? They'd looked like they were up to something. She was putting the key into her door when she heard heavy footsteps on the stairs behind her. She turned just as Dan Dawson came around the corner of the landing. He was dressed all in black from the Stetson covering his black hair to his boots. All the black made his blue eyes stand out.

The man was gorgeous.

He swept his hat off and held it in one hand. "Hello, Ash," he said, his lips twisting into a lazy smile that made his eyes look dreamy. Or maybe they just made Ashby feel dreamy when they caught her with her guard down.

"Hello," she said, though her throat had gone dry. "How are you?" She meant both emotionally and physically. She wondered if he'd stopped coughing.

"I'm good." He patted his chest. "Stopped coughing a couple of days ago. Thanks for taking such good care of me. I should have come by sooner."

He'd come to thank her. The idea pleased her. "I was glad to. Everyone is about to burst, they're so ready to get out there tomorrow and start cleaning up."

He nodded. "They're good people. You coming, too?"

She felt her stomach flutter when his smile seemed

to reach out and touch her. She nodded, making him smile briefly.

"I'll look forward to seeing you there and getting the place cleaned up. I've been stuck trying to get a list ready for the insurance company."

Feeling awkward just standing there, Ashby placed her hand on the door frame. She didn't trust herself to move her hand farther to pat his shoulder. "I'm really sorry. I know it's hard."

He tapped the hat on his thigh, his expression thoughtful. "Like the Bible says, we came into this world with nothing and we'll leave with nothing."

"This is true. Still, it has to hurt some." Ashby realized he didn't look devastated.

His lips thinned and he met her eyes straight-on. "I learned a long time ago that there are some things you can't control. And the secret to not letting them have control over you is simply not to let them. If you understand what's important, it's not so hard to do that. Now, if someone had died in that fire, then I'd have lost something. The most I lost was a bunch of furniture."

"You do realize you could have been killed running in, right? But I understand. If someone thought there was a reasonable chance of getting back out, they would have done the same."

"I felt pretty good about it when I went in. But I also know, as much as I hate to think about not having a photo of my mom, even if that had burned up, I'd still have her in my heart."

Ashby was touched. She and Dan had never had a serious conversation before. Even the day they'd spent getting through the bike race, they'd been too busy butting heads. "I'm glad you have the picture. How long has your mother been gone?"

"About six years. She was a remarkable lady."

Esther Mae's words fluttered through Ashby's mind. "You'll have to tell me about her sometime."

He smiled. "I just might do that."

Their eyes locked and held. Ashby smiled. "Well, I have to go. I need to change. Are you looking for someone in the apartment building?"

"Nope, I'm just checking out my new digs."

Ashby met his twinkling eyes. "New digs?"

He jerked his head toward the door behind him. "My new apartment for the next few months."

Nothing could have surprised Ashby more. "You're moving in? Here?" She sounded as dumb as a brick.

"Yep," he said, and winked. "Howdy, neighbor."

Chapter Eight

It had been a tough week, but Dan had made it. He'd stayed at Clint and Lacy's for five nights, and had tossed around several ideas about his living arrangements for the next few months. When Adela had called and offered the free use of the vacant apartment in her complex, he'd liked the idea immediately. He'd insisted on paying, of course. She looked fragile, but she'd been a hard sell. Even after he'd explained that his insurance policy reimbursed him for housing while he rebuilt, she'd held out, refusing to take payment. In the end, they'd settled on her donating the rental fee to the women's shelter. Both of them had been happy with that solution.

It wasn't until he'd climbed the stairs and encountered Ashby that he realized there might be an added benefit to living here. He wouldn't get bored, that was for certain. Not that he'd be around all that much. Still, he had to admit that he found the idea appealing. Much more appealing than camping out in his barn, which he had been thinking about doing before Adela approached him about the apartment. He could have stayed at Clint's but it might be five months before his place was finished. That was too long to impose on his friend's generosity.

Looking at Ashby's stunned expression, he knew she didn't share his feelings. The idea bothered him. "Hey, you just told me how good it was to see me."

She paled. "Oh, uh, yes. I mean, it's great that you're moving in."

Dan found her completely lovely in her pink, flustered state. Yes indeed, this could be very appealing. He pulled his key from his pocket. "Do you want to take a look with me?"

"No, really. I need to go. I have to get ready for Max's birthday party—"

"Hey, I'm going to the party, too." He stuck the key in and let the door swing open. "Come on. Take a quick tour. You can give me the insider's perspective." He could see her waffling, so he tried a pitiful expression to win her over.

She relented. "A quick tour, then."

"After you." He stepped back and let her pass.

"You're going to need everything," she said as soon as they were inside the bare apartment.

"Not really. I'll probably just get the basics. Something to sleep on and a chair. Maybe a cooking pot." He was surprised when she whirled around to face him. She was beautiful in her concern, her big emerald eyes wide.

"You'll do no such thing! I'm sure everyone will want to pitch in and help furnish the place for you."

"Ash, it's okay. I was just joking. A little, anyway. I'll get a frying pan, too." The woman did not know how to take a joke.

Her eyes glittered as she clamped her mouth shut. "This is the kitchen." She swung her arm wide, encompassing the small galley kitchen with its oak cabinets and white appliances. Then she pushed past him and stormed to the door off the living room. "This is your bathroom, and here—" she took a step back, to the second door "—is the bedroom. And there you have it. Small but cozy. I'm sure you and your cooking pot will be very happy."

"Does it make you mad that I can joke?"

She crossed her arms in a huff, making her hair swing at her jaw. "Yes, actually, it does. I think you hurt more than you are admitting, and, like always, you hide behind this jokey facade."

Their eyes met and held for a moment. "You think I live a lie?"

She looked away for an instant. "Well, not necessarily a lie. But I think you—"

"You don't know me well enough to even begin to understand what I think, Ash. You judge me, but you won't even try to get to know me."

"You're right," she said, moving to the door. "I don't know you. And I certainly don't understand you. And

I think you've reminded me of that fact a couple of times now."

"Only because I keep hoping maybe somewhere along the way you might want to get to know me better."

"And I told you before that wouldn't work. It would be a waste of time for both of us. I'm really sorry for what's happened, but nothing else has changed between us."

She left him standing in the center of his new apartment. The woman flashed fire through her eyes sometimes when he said something she disagreed with. It was intense enough to make everything else fade when it happened. And there was no use explaining it away…

"You do know I'm not a guy who gives up easily," he called after her. "Especially on a worthwhile cause."

The slam of her door made him chuckle.

This could be a very interesting setup.

The actual celebration for Max was that several of the men were taking him, his best friend, Gil, who lived down the road, and a few guys from school camping. Rose had suggested it, but wanted to have cake and sodas before the guys headed out.

Ashby was on a soda restocking mission in the kitchen when Dan came striding in. She'd watched him strut around, flirting easily with all the ladies, especially Stacy, and she'd witnessed firsthand how they all reacted to him. Why, even Stacy, who didn't talk much to anyone, spoke to Dan. She had actually seemed relaxed with him. That never happened, not even when she was in a roomful of women. Ashby wasn't sure if this was good or bad, but she had to admit it was remarkable.

As if they hadn't argued earlier, he smiled when he saw her. "I've been sent to help you." He held out his arms. "Load me up. I'm yours."

She hadn't yet forgotten the earnest look in his eyes when he'd told her he hoped she'd want to get to know him. She'd even felt tempted to change her ways, until she arrived here to find him already in action.

Tearing her eyes away from his smile, she hurried over to the ice chest. It was packed full of a variety of drinks. "Can you lift this?" she asked, glancing at him coolly.

The expression that crossed his face was comical, a mixture of insult and disbelief. She did not have to hear his voice to know his ego was stung by the question. Dan lifted his arm and did a quick bicep curl, a purely male response that almost made her want to smile.

"What do you think?" There was a teasing gleam in his eyes.

"I guess a silly question deserves a silly answer."

His shotgun laugh startled her with its intensity; she felt it all the way to the soles of her feet.

He cocked his head to the side. "I'm going to win you over if it's the last thing I do, Ashby Templeton."

The entire incident flustered Ashby so badly she was certain he could see she wasn't as immune to him as she wanted to be. "I wouldn't be too sure about that." She hoped she sounded more confident than she suddenly felt.

Of course, he winked at her. Which should have reminded her that this was a game to him.

But it didn't matter to her. And that was the scary part. "Can I help you?" she asked. Needing a distraction, she reached for one handle of the chest.

"Sure. I would say tell me how to win you over. But actually, I like the challenge of figuring you out."

Despite her frustration, her lips twitched. "You never give up, do you?"

He turned serious in a flash. "I think for the first time since I've known you, you finally got something right about me, Ash. I never give up."

It was said with such conviction that she believed him. After a heartbeat, he winked again, picked up the loaded ice chest as if it were a five-pound bag of sugar and strode out the door.

She stood where he'd left her, in the middle of the roomy kitchen, heart thundering in her chest, her stomach bottomless. Excitement. Anticipation. Danger…that's what she was feeling.

And she'd be lying if she said she didn't like it.

"You look a little flustered," Rose said as Ashby came to stand beside her. "I saw Dan bring out the cooler of drinks. Does he have anything to do with those pink cheeks?"

"The man completely baffles me. It's frustrating."

"You know, girlfriend, that's not a bad thing," Lacy interjected. She laughed when Ashby appeared less than convinced. “Keeping your sweetie on his toes, and vice versa, keeps the sparks flying.”

“Okay, enough of that. I want to fall in love and have children, but I want it to be long-term, and Dan is a short-term kinda man. Believe me, I know. *That’s* what those sparks are all about.”

Rose and Lacy each laid a hand on her arm. Rose spoke. “I know what you mean. I had dreams just as strong as yours, and I understand where you are coming from. But I think you’re reading this wrong. I think Dan is a forever man. I think he’s the type of guy who falls once, hard, and hangs on without letting go. He’s a good man, Ashby. If you watch him, really watch the way he interacts with women and children, you might see more to him than you think. He’s never been anything but respectful to me.”

Ashby found him in the middle of the crowd of boys, playing football. He was running across the field with three of them hanging off him, laughing as he went. The admiration on the boys’ adolescent faces was apparent. He wasn’t letting them win easily, and Ashby realized the boys were eating it up.

“Dan is in no hurry to fall in love. It could be years before he wants a family. I’m ready now. Believe me, I’ve wasted enough years of my life on men who aren’t ready to commit. I don’t have time to get mixed up with another man like that.” She didn’t feel like elaborating.

Steven had been just as charming, just as carefree and just as openly flirtatious as Dan. She’d fallen in love with him against her better judgment, and look where it got her. In the end, he'd found he couldn't be a one-woman man, which left Ashby out in the cold. She couldn't go through that again. It wasn't just Steven—almost every guy she'd dated had the Peter Pan syndrome. They were completely content to remain in Never-Never Land for eternity. Like Dan. He was happy with the way he was. She had to wonder if he would ever grow up and take on the responsibility of a family. Despite what Lacy and Rose thought about him, she couldn't trust him.

"I'm looking for a man more like Lance Yates."

Lacy's mouth fell open. "Lance Yates? Give me a break. He's nice and all, but I saw you two talking at the last potluck dinner—there wasn't so much as a flicker in your eye when you looked at him. Not the case with our man Dan. You should see your eyes fire up when you look at that man. Pretty telling, if you ask me. And anyway, men fall when they fall. When that love bug hits, girl, there's not one thing you can do about it."

Ashby wasn't so sure about that—sparks in her eyes or men suddenly falling in love and everything changing. No, men like Steven didn't change. She'd stay away from his kind. Because to do otherwise meant a broken heart.

She watched Dan as he went down beneath his tenacious assailants. They all landed hard, a pile of tangled legs and arms, with Dan on the bottom. It hit her that the man would be good with children.

"Max loves it when Dan comes out here," Rose said, as if reading her thoughts.

Ashby smoothed her slacks and tried to look as if that bit of information didn't surprise her. She also had to fight off asking why and when. She spent at least three or four evenings a month here babysitting, and she'd never seen him.

She felt eyes on her and looked up to find both Rose and Lacy smiling at her like hyenas.

Ashby fumbled for a topic, any topic other than the one they so obviously were dying to discuss as they continued to study her. She felt like a lab rat. "Oh, what's the use? I guess you both already know he's moving in next door to me."

They both laughed out loud. "We've been wondering when you were going to say something," Lacy said.

"We didn't want to push too hard," Rose admitted.

"For some reason I find that hard to believe." Ashby smiled, despite the turmoil inside her. "Please don't give the ladies false hope."

"Ashby," Lacy huffed. "They aren't listening to us."

She knew it was true. Still, she hoped if no one else made a big deal out of it, they'd let it go. She was going to have a hard enough time dealing with Dan himself, without worrying about anyone else pushing them together. And she was afraid that if she didn't keep up her guard she might give in and go out with him. She hated to admit it, but she was already weakening. She was going to have to do a lot of praying on this. God had a plan for her life, she knew He did. She just had to be patient. But that was exactly the problem. She'd lost her patience a long time ago. She wanted a family. And she was terrified God might tell her no.

Because of that fear, she'd made some wrong choices when it came to men. Steven hadn't been her first mistake. She'd been trying not to disappoint her mother when she'd wasted time dating Carlton and Brad. She hadn't liked either of them in the first place, but knew they were the type of affluent men her mother wanted her to marry. Men with blood so blue it sparkled. Or so her mother thought. Their rejections had been a blessing, because she realized if she'd married either of them it wouldn't have been right. Of course, it had taken her a few rejections to find it in herself to stop trying to please her mother. Her mother would have been happy with either marriage, but Ashby would have been miserable. Still, even this understanding hadn't prevented the damage caused to her self-esteem over their rejection. For a girl who'd been brought up to think keeping up with the Joneses was everything, being told twice in a row you didn't was hard.

And that was when Steven had shown up. No, fear of not pleasing her mother and fear of the Lord not giving her the family she so desperately wanted had cost her dearly. She wasn't going to let anything sidetrack her from finding the right man this time. She might feel completely desperate, but she would make herself be patient. That required discipline. It required her not to let Dan Dawson's boyish charm through the chinks in her armor.

* * *

There was nothing like taking one ten-year-old and five thirteen- and fourteen-year-olds camping. Dan had grown up without a father, and he understood all too well how important it was for the men of the church to step up and be there for boys like Max. Brady did what he could, but he worked long hours, and soon he and Dottie would have a baby of their own.

The women's shelter was in what had been Brady's home, which he'd donated when he'd moved to a smaller place on the family property. It gave him and Dottie some privacy, as opposed to living at the shelter full-time. It also freed up space for women in need.

As the campfire flickered, Dan watched the boys listening intently to Clint tell about his run-in with a group of cattle rustlers.

Dan thought about Stacy. She had started coming out of her shell. Talking to people was getting easier for her. She had even looked him in the eye earlier that afternoon. It happened more and more frequently. When those crystal-clear gray eyes met his and held, even if only for two seconds, he wanted to shout "Hallelujah!" It had taken him months of diligent, steady work and countless trips to the candy store to gain her trust. Regaining trust took time. It wasn't anything he took lightly. It had been the same way for his mother all those years ago after she'd braved the wrath of her husband by escaping with Dan to a safe house. Dan remembered the beatings as if they were yesterday, and knew he probably owed his life to his mother.

She'd broken the cycle of violence and given him a chance to become a man whose life wasn't ruled by violence, but by compassion. Still, he was deeply aware of the statistic that boys raised in abusive homes had a greater risk of becoming abusive themselves. It was always at the back of his mind. Looking at Max, a healthy, happy kid, Dan wondered how desperate the situation had been for him and Rose before they'd gotten out. Though Rose was doing a great job, he prayed for Max to one day have a new dad.

He also prayed for Stacy. She was just as heavy on his heart. With God's help and guidance, one day she would be able to hold her head high with confidence. Dan's heart was burdened with an urge to help the residents of No Place Like Home.

His thoughts turned to his new neighbor. She didn't trust him. She truly thought he was a no-good flirt. He *was* a flirt—guilty as charged. But that was a tool to plant friendship and trust with the ladies at No Place Like Home.

It was a part of him that he would never change, yet never explain, either. And it was part of the problem with Ashby.

Not just because the idea of revealing something so personal didn't set well with him. It went deeper than that. Became more complicated. He was who he was, and Ashby, like everyone else he'd ever met, would have to take him or leave him based on what they saw in him.

In his view, people who didn't look past their prejudices and preconceived notions didn't deserve an explanation of who he was at his core.

Besides, his actions involving women and children who'd been hurt were deliberate, prayed-up actions with a mission. They were his ministry.

He believed everyone had a path. A heaven-ordained path where every good thing and every bad thing a person went through would be used for the benefit of God's kingdom. He'd strayed and stumbled along the way trying to completely separate himself from his past. Hoping to rid himself of haunting memories that he'd thought lingered because of his volunteering at the shelters. After all, with his mother's guidance, they'd been volunteering at them for years. So his thinking had been that some distance would help lay the past to rest. During that time, he'd moved to Mule Hollow, a quiet little town out in the middle of nowhere. Of course, God had opened his eyes when No Place Like Home relocated out here beside him. This time his involvement was wholehearted.

He just didn't feel compelled to share that. It was almost as if sharing it would diminish it….

He'd been a kid with a no-good dad and an extraordinary mother. Looking back over his life, Dan saw that God's hand was clearly visible in the events that had happened to him. But if he opened up, revealed that, it would seem as if he were trying to take the focus off God and put it on himself.

People who looked closely enough would see a pattern, but if he talked about it, the element of humility would disappear.

And though he didn't think anyone would believe it about him, being humble was what he liked the best.

Chapter Nine

Things were not good. On Saturday morning Ashby's mother called. Her unhappy mother. Ashby's picture was on the Internet....

In conjunction with her weekly newspaper column, Molly Jacobs had a Web site that attracted a good number of avid readers who enjoyed hearing about small-town life in Mule Hollow. Molly was able to share far more on the Web site than she was in the paper. And it was there Molly had posted her pictures of the pig scramble.

"You look horrid! Just horrid!" her mother exclaimed the instant Ashby said hello.

It was a phrase Ashby had heard too many times through the years to recount. She'd come to realize it meant her mother was nervous, and not that Ashby necessarily looked horrid.

Lydia had obviously been to Molly's Web site and

seen photos of her daughter's run-in with the pig. So today when she used the word *horrid,* she meant it.

Ashby had actually thought about doing bodily harm to Molly when she'd realized the photos had been uploaded. She'd checked them out before going to bed last night and had been mortified. Thankfully, her mug shot was in a collage with several others. Harmless, right? That was what she'd told herself as she'd tried to go to sleep.

Until this moment, though, listening to her mother's hysterics on the phone, she hadn't been sure that Lydia was actually keeping up with what went on in Mule Hollow. It wasn't as if Ashby made the papers all that much.

"Calm down, Mother."

"How can you expect me to calm down when all my friends will be seeing *this!*"

The rebellious side of Ashby wanted to remind her that a lady did not screech, scream or raise her voice. Nor did she surf the Web looking for compromising images of her daughter. But Ashby didn't. At times like this, she felt like the little girl in the pink taffeta party dress who'd just embarrassed her mother at Agatha Hathaway's seventh birthday party. Even at six years old, Ashby had recognized the humiliation in her mother's eyes…and hated knowing she'd put it there. Despite the fact that she'd purposefully poured the red punch down her dress, knowing it would bother her mother. She just hadn't expected how ashamed it would make her. That was the day Ashby started denying the rebellious child inside her and began trying to make her mother proud of her.

It had taken years to realize that was an unattainable goal. Lydia loved her in her own complicated way, and that had to be enough.

"Your friends in Pacific Heights won't even know it's me," Ashby said now, happy that Molly hadn't tagged names to individual photos. The entire grouping bore the label "A fun time at the pig scramble for the ladies of Mule Hollow." Thank goodness for small blessings.

"I can only hope that's true. However, a *pig scramble*—Ashby, that's pushing the limits of good taste. From the picture, it's obvious you were wallowing in the dirt with that animal. Surely, even you can see my point in this."

The acid in her stomach churning, Ashby closed her eyes and prayed the Lord would give her patience. "Yes, Mother, I understand completely. I apologize for any embarrassment I may have caused you." She knew there was nothing else that would appease her mother.

"Very well. I must go. I'm presenting at the garden club this afternoon and I have much to do."

"Enjoy yourself, Mother." Ashby's fingers tightened around the handset. There was a brief pause before the line went dead. Holding the silent phone, Ashby fought to regain her footing, longing for a closeness with her mom that she knew she would never have.

One day she would have her own child...and things

would be different. Her arms ached to hold her baby, and her heart longed to show it the love she'd always craved for herself.

She blinked hard against the threat of tears. God must let her have a child.

By the time Ashby made it out to Dan's place, cleanup was in full swing. It looked like anyone who didn't have to work was here offering a helping hand. As she got out of her car, she shielded her eyes from the glare of the sun and tried to decide where she should start. Esther Mae, Adela and a few of the younger ladies had formed an assembly line of sorts. They were taking items such as flatware from a pile of salvaged goods and scrubbing them down. Ashby saw overalls-clad Norma Sue poking around in the ruins with a hoe. Several cowboys were doing the same, trying to see if anything of value survived in the ashes.

Her gaze settled on Dan, who was walking around with Will Sutton. Will had a business creating beautiful, artistic iron gates, but he also happened to be an architect. Ashby surveyed the damage. Most of the outer walls were a combination of brick and limestone and they were still standing, but the majority of the wood framework was either charred or completely burned. Many interior walls were gone, the roof was missing and rubble covered the concrete foundation. It was a disaster.

The good news was that Dan had insurance. Though

items with sentimental value were a loss, he would come out of this with a new home. At least that was how the local grapevine had it. Ashby hadn't talked with him personally about it beyond their brief conversation the day before.

Dan seemed to have his head on straight when it came to material possessions. She couldn't really say whether, if her place burned, there would be much she would be heartbroken about losing. Still, Ashby suspected there would be emotional effects from the ordeal. Then again, as Dan had said, the crucial thing would be that no one was hurt in the fire.

They might have their differences, but she loved his perspective on what was important in life.

Over the past few days, she'd started to realize Dan Dawson actually had layers she hadn't seen before.

"Hey, Ashby!" Lacy poked her head out from behind a half wall that had hidden her from view. She had soot across one cheek and portions of her pale hair had black tips. At her exclamation, everyone looked up and greeted Ashby. Dan smiled and made his way over to where she stood.

"You did come to join the party," he said warmly.

"I would have been out sooner, but I had to work until noon." She reminded herself that he smiled like this at all women. And that his eyes twinkled naturally.

"I'm glad you came."

"So, what should I do?" Ashby asked Dan, ignoring the way her stomach flipped when he was near.

"You could help over there, maybe." He waved toward the washing line. "I wouldn't advise coming in here. I've been trying to get the ladies to stay on that side of the site because of nails and other hazards. As you can see, there are two who have ignored me."

"Hey, I heard that," Lacy called, peeking back over the wall.

"I did, too," Norma Sue shouted from the back corner of the house. "I'll have you know I can look out for a nail as good as any man can. Being a woman doesn't make me blind."

Dan chuckled and looked sheepish. "Can't do a thing with those two. It's a mess in here, though, so I would feel better if you didn't cross the threshold."

"Ashby, you can come in here and help me," Lacy called. Obviously, she had supersonic hearing.

Curious about what her friend was doing, and ready to put some space between herself and Dan, Ashby stepped into the ruins despite his wishes. "I'll be careful," she said when his brows dipped with worry.

"Okay, but watch yourself." He took her arm as she stepped over a burned ceiling beam, and continued to grasp her elbow as she skirted water-damaged debris.

Ashby wasn't sure why they thought anything could be salvaged. The whole place was a disaster. She glanced up to find Dan watching her.

"I know what you're thinking. I tried to tell them it was hopeless." He shrugged. "No one is paying any attention to anything I say. What's a man to do?"

His whipped-puppy expression made her chuckle again. "Poor baby. I guess you'll just have to humor them." Her teasing surprised her and elicited a smile in return.

"Why, Miss Templeton, I do believe you just made a joke."

"Yes, I did," she said. "And now *I* need to get busy, so don't let me keep you from what you were doing."

"Okay, but really, be careful." He sauntered off in that easy gait that was pure Dan.

Ashby squatted down beside Lacy. "What are you doing?"

Lacy showed her the pile of ash she was digging through. "I'm finding Dan's mother's jewelry." With her free hand, she reached into her shirt pocket and pulled out a smoke-blackened necklace.

Ashby gasped, watching Lacy tuck it back into her pocket. "He didn't have it in a safe-deposit box?"

"Men. They don't think! He told me he kept her jewelry box in a drawer of his dresser. So I'm just digging around. I've found a necklace and a bracelet. They may be ruined beyond repair, but I feel good trying to salvage them for him. He said though she didn't have a lot of it, he'd planned on giving it to his children someday. If he had any."

Ashby started to poke around in the grimy mix of ash and burned items. Until yesterday, she hadn't even pictured Dan with children. But watching him play with the boys at the party had awakened her to the fact that he would be a good father if he ever decided to settle down. Which would be *years,* she reminded herself. Even he had tagged on *if* he had any to his statement.

"Oh!" She felt positively giddy when she realized the black oval she was looking at was a ring. Picking it up, she held it in her palm and studied it.

"Is it a wedding band?" Lacy asked, just as excited.

"Maybe. There doesn't appear to be any stones on it. Here, tuck it in there with the other pieces and let's keep going. I might turn into a treasure hunter yet. We could even rent a metal detector before the bulldozers come in and take it all down." If Dan's mother had been anything like hers, there could be a truckload of jewelry in this pile of ash.

"Nope." Lacy shook her head. "He said she had two rings, a bracelet and three necklaces. So we're almost done. One more each is all."

Ashby found herself curious about the woman who inspired that devotion. "He really loved his mother, didn't he?" Their voices were hushed, both of them aware how their words could carry.

"I think they had a hard life. He doesn't speak about it. I was talking once about how hard it was sometimes without my dad in the picture for me and my mother, and Dan got this really sympathetic look on his face. He said something I've never forgotten—that it gave us an unbreakable bond. He understood, I could tell. He's never been one to talk much about his past, so it makes me curious. Ya know what I mean?" She'd been digging in the ashes and now sent Ashby a sideways smile.

Ashby pointed at the ground. "Stop it, and dig!"

Her friend laughed. "Okay, but you aren't fooling me. I know you noticed. And I know you're curious, too."

She was, Ashby thought, glancing over at him. But she didn't want to be.

"Whoo-hoo and glory be!" Norma Sue shouted suddenly. "*Pictures!* Y'all come look."

Everyone made their way over to where the woman stood, with a Texas-size grin plastered on her face. Beside her was what looked like a two-foot pile of ashes.

"I went to rake these up and the drawer front just fell off."

Dan reached into the cavity and pulled out the picture album Norma Sue had revealed. It was covered in soot, but when he opened the cover, the pictures inside were safe. "Would you look at that," he said as he turned the pages. There was awe in his tone and his expression.

Ashby felt her throat tighten with emotion, overwhelmed by the moment. He'd regained another connection to the past, which, yes, she was becoming more and more curious about. When he closed the book and engulfed Norma Sue in a bear hug, Ashby's heart was touched.

Tugging at his mustache, Norma Sue's husband turned and surveyed the disaster. "I wonder how many more of these here piles have surprises in them."

An almost electric excitement infected everyone as they surveyed the heaps of ashes and debris.

"Let's get digging," Lacy exclaimed, and with renewed energy, everyone set to work once more.

Ashby met Dan's gaze as she started to turn away, and she smiled at him. And for the first time since she'd known him, it felt totally sincere.

Chapter Ten

Dan stood at the end of the walk at Adela's apartment house and surveyed the trucks waiting to be unloaded. He'd been blessed by the goodness of the community he lived in. Not only had folks spent all day today salvaging some of his belongings from the fire, but now they were donating things from their own homes for him to use in his temporary apartment. There would be no need for him to use money on furnishings until he was ready to move back into his house. Everything he could possibly need was here: couch and chair, bed, dresser, a box of cooking utensils, sheets and a spread. There was even a telephone sitting on top of one box.

"Y'all didn't need to go to all this trouble," he said to the beaming group before him.

"Sure we did," Norma Sue said. "What are friends for if not to help out in situations like this?"

"You would have done the same," Clint said, letting

the tailgate down and hopping up into the back of his truck. "Now, if you'll just grab that end, we'll get this couch upstairs."

"I'll get the door," Ashby called, and headed up the steps. Dan watched her go, then grabbed the end of the beige couch. He'd found himself watching her off and on all afternoon. She'd worked hard, looking for anything in the ashes that might be cleaned up. Though they hadn't found much other than the picture album and the jewelry, he viewed both as an act of God. How else could they have survived? The townspeople weren't aware that he'd been through this once before, when he and his mother left their home in the middle of the night with nothing but the clothes on their backs. He understood things were only things. But when Ashby had placed the soot-covered jewelry in his palm, he'd realized how much it meant to him. He'd found himself choked up as he gazed down at the items.

When he looked up to find Ashby watching him, he'd been startled by the expression of understanding he saw in her eyes. He'd felt a connection with her in that moment. The rest of the day they both stayed busy. While she'd really dug in and worked as hard as anyone, he'd caught her watching him sometimes...caught her because he'd been watching her most of the time. And though it might have been wishful thinking on his part, he thought she might finally have begun to see him in a better light.

"Be careful and don't trip," Esther Mae called, bringing his thoughts back to the moment at hand. He backed up the path, glad he hadn't tripped while his mind wandered.

"This is a great couch, Clint," he said, stepping up onto the porch before angling the heavy sofa through the doorway.

"It was mine before Lacy and I got married. I don't know if you've noticed, but my wife isn't into neutral tones."

Dan laughed. "That's for sure." Lacy wore some of the brightest clothes he'd ever seen. Not only had she painted her salon hot-pink, but she'd inspired others to become creative, to the point that Mule Hollow was starting to look like a rainbow. "I can't picture this tan couch, as nice as it is, in a home with Lacy."

"Yup, she said that it was the perfect couch for a bachelor. Hope you don't mind if I sneak over every once in a while to visit it."

Dan was backing up the steps now, and he paused to glance down at Clint. The man's happy marriage was inspiring to a guy like Dan, who'd lived in such a messed-up home. "You are welcome anytime, but somehow I don't think you'll miss it."

The couch wasn't going to fit.

Ashby shook her head and watched as a cute and frustrated Dan, with the help of Clint, wrestled with the sofa. It wasn't going in, not the way they were trying to manhandle it through the doorway. To be fair to the couch, it wasn't the width that was the problem. She thought she'd found a solution, but Dan was so entertaining in his macho determination to impress her that she couldn't bear to interrupt. And impress her was clearly what he was trying to do. She was actually enjoying watching the way his forehead creased with consternation.

The hallway had long since grown congested with people waiting to carry their armloads into the apartment, and suggestions began to ring out.

Norma Sue suggested standing it up on end. That didn't work.

Esther Mae pointed at them with the floor lamp she was carrying and recommended taking the door off. "That's what we had to do last year getting my new hutch into the kitchen. I thought Hank was going to blow a gasket on that one."

Hank grunted. "She's not telling a story on that. I was ready to haul that hunk of wood back to the antique store. Pronto."

Ashby couldn't stand it any longer. "Try turning it upside down."

"Upside down?" Dan asked.

He was standing close to her, since he'd set the couch down to study the doorway, and she realized she was enjoying his nearness more than she wanted. "It's a different dynamic like that. Flip it upside down and then angle it. I think it'll work."

He looked from her to Clint. "It's worth a try."

They picked it up again, and Ashby and Lacy grabbed the cushions. With Ashby directing them on the right way to angle the couch, they walked it through the door, no problem at all.

"Well, what do you know." Esther Mae harrumphed. "Look, Hank, all you had to do was turn my hutch upside down!"

Everyone laughed when he rolled his eyes.

"Thanks, neighbor." Dan grinned at Ashby and was rewarded with a smile. "So, you got it in here. Now where should I put it?" He and Clint stopped in the center of the small living room.

His midnight eyes met Ashby's. "Come on, don't be shy. I know you have an opinion. Don't you watch those shows on television that tell you how to do all this kind of stuff?"

"No, I don't. But set it here," Ashby said, pointing at the floor in front of her. "This way the couch will act as a partition to the traffic coming from the doorway and the other rooms of the place. We'll put the chair there, and the television in that corner. Don't you agree, Lacy?"

She nodded, coming around the bar from the kitchen. "Move it, boys." She clapped her hands, grinning at them.

Dan and Clint picked the couch up from where they'd set it between them and placed it where Ashby indicated. Then they backed away and studied their handiwork. "A woman's touch is a good thing," Dan said. "I may have to get you to help me when my new place is ready. I'd have had all the chairs and the couch up against the walls."

"My furniture is up against the walls," Esther Mae

said, as she stepped out of the bedroom. "Oh, I like that. I see what y'all mean." She stared at the couch critically. "I want you and Lacy to come out to my place to rearrange my furniture."

"There's nothing wrong with couches up against the wall," Ashby protested. "But if that's what you want, we'll come."

Dan and Clint exchanged looks. *Women.*

"This will be fun," Lacy said, leading the way out the door for another load.

"Not for me," Hank groaned, following his wife. "That means I'll be hitting my toes on table legs when I get up in the dark."

"You'll live," Esther Mae said, shooting him an arch look over her shoulder. "We're outdated and these girls can bring us up to par."

Everyone trailed out the door, chattering as they went. Ashby and Dan brought up the rear.

He studied her as they walked shoulder to shoulder down the stairs. He was enjoying himself immensely.

"I like your way," he said. "The place is going to look homey." He was a guy. It didn't really matter to him all that much, but he figured there was nothing wrong with things looking the best they could. Especially if it meant being around Ashby. They were alone at the bottom of the stairs and he stopped. "I might have to cook you dinner to show my appreciation."

Ashby looked at him with a twinkle in her eyes. "Maybe you will."

Dan was so surprised by her positive answer that he made the biggest mistake ever—he kissed her.

Pull away. Walk away, the leftovers of Ashby's sane brain were screaming, as Dan lowered his lips to hers but…his lips were firm, unhesitant and oh, so wonderful.

As he pulled her close, his heart pounded next to hers. When his arms settled securely about her, with such practiced perfection, Ashby really wanted more than anything to pull away—but she was trapped. Trapped by the fact that his kiss was perfect, and so achingly sweet, Ashby felt as if she were floating…. How could she possibly pull away from such bliss—

"Hallelujah! I told you love was in the air!"

At the sound of Esther Mae's gushing exclamation, Ashby yanked herself out of Dan's arms, stumbling up against the wall. What had she done? She grabbed the banister for courage as much as for support. Not only was Esther Mae standing in the doorway, but Norma Sue and Adela, as well. All three were beaming at her with delight.

"Esther Mae, don't jump to conclusions," Adela warned, overcoming the astonishment she and the others must have felt, coming upon Ashley and Dan locked in an embrace.

Ashby pushed all thoughts about it out of her mind. She was mortified, barely able to glance at Dan. He, on the other hand, was tickled pink. Literally. She looked closer at him, and found the cowboy's sun-bronzed skin was actually looking flushed.

Ashby wanted to wring his neck. She did, she really did.

But that wouldn't do at all.

Chapter Eleven

"Now, ladies, don't get your hopes up. That was just a friendly thank-you kiss to Ash for all her help today." Dan had messed up royally, and he was trying as calmly as he knew how to deter the matchmaking fervor before him.

But his head was fuzzy and Ashby was as purple as an overripe plum. He understood that perfectly, since it was about two hundred degrees where he was standing.

"I suddenly have a pain in my head," she muttered between clenched teeth "If you'll excuse me, I'm sure you can finish this without me."

Dan's temperature plummeted as he and everyone else watched her march stiffly up the stairs. Okay, he'd been right; he had messed up.

Just when he'd thought he had changed her perception of him, he'd gone and lost his good sense. He should have backed away the moment he realized he was going to kiss her.

But he hadn't been thinking—she'd just looked so cute accepting his dinner invitation, or at least alluding to it. He'd reacted out of his astonishment and kissed her. And she'd kissed him back. True, the minute his lips had touched hers and she'd responded so sweetly, he'd not been thinking about anything but how perfect she felt in his arms…when he should have been realizing she was just startled by his reaction. After all, she might have been totally teasing him and hadn't expected some overbearing oaf to kiss her! What a jerk he was—he didn't normally lose control of the situation, but where Ashby was concerned, he didn't seem to be in control at all anymore.

The overbearing, too-confident-for-his-own-good cowboy had kissed her, then acted as if it was no big deal.

And it wasn't. That's what she told herself as she scrubbed her kitchen counter. The sink. And again as she started on the cabinets of her already spotless kitchen. Seething, she glanced at the brass clock hanging over the stove. It had been exactly three hours since he'd kissed her. Three hours. The ill-mannered, uncouth man hadn't apologized yet, proving every bad thing she'd thought about him.

She knew the man was full of himself, but to just kiss her out of the blue like that showed a deeper lack of consideration than she'd expected from him, given the fact that she'd expressed her concern. His audacity was mind-boggling. And to think she was going to have to live beside him for weeks. Maybe months!

You kissed him back.

Ashby felt sick. She had. She really, really had kissed him back.

Truth was, for an instant before his lips touched hers, she'd wanted to kiss him. She had and, well, there was just no getting around it. Maybe it was her mother's phone call that morning. Maybe it was all these rebellious feelings cavorting around inside her, like balls in a bingo cage.

You kissed him back. And that was what really bothered her.

She scrubbed harder even as she tried to tell herself to relax, that it was only a kiss. A light touching of the lips—it really had been nothing. But that was hard to do when she could still feel the impression of his lips as if he'd branded her.

Goodness.

This was ridiculous. It wasn't as if she hadn't been kissed before. So what was the big deal?

Face it, despite everything, you are attracted to Dan!

She flung her cleaning rag into the sink and stared out the kitchen window. She *shouldn't* be attracted to him.

Why?

He was a playboy, and the ungentlemanly kiss proved it.

Maybe not.

Men like him couldn't be trusted. He wasn't the man for her.

She needed to put him out of her head, get back on

track and forget any of this had happened. Forget that she'd enjoyed spending time with him today. Forget that there were things about him she liked. Forget that when he looked at her, she felt like a girl again.

Ashby hung her head and took a deep, shuddering breath. For her it was all a fool's trail.

A shower would make her feel better, she decided, looking down at her clothes. It had been a long day. Feeling hopeful that she could wash the confusion out of her head, she walked down the hall to her bedroom.

A few minutes later, grit-free after a wonderful hot shower, she felt a bit more optimistic. Clad in her favorite mint-toned silk pajamas and matching wrap, she was heading back into the bedroom when she decided tonight would be a good night for a calming seaweed mask as she relaxed with her Bible study.

Turning back to the bathroom, she opened her cabinet and looked at the toiletry items lined up in perfect rows. Snatching a tube, she applied the contents in a thick layer. The lovely scent of mint enveloped her. "Nice, normal routine," she told her reflection, noting how the seaweed mask on her face matched her silk wrap. Feeling more relaxed, she padded barefoot into the kitchen and poured herself a glass of grape juice. By the time she settled into bed, propped against her fluffed pillows with her Bible opened on her lap, she was feeling like herself again.

Ashby found the place in Philippians where she'd left off the night before, and started reading. With the discontent she'd been feeling, she'd had to be diligent in her Bible study of late. She wanted to trust the Lord even when she wasn't happy with her life, and it wasn't always easy to do. During times like this, she needed the Lord to speak to her through scriptures more than ever. She needed to be reminded that she wasn't alone in her struggles. Even Bible heroes and heroines had had times when they weren't completely satisfied....

Realizing that her mind had wandered from the verses in front of her, Ashby took a sip of grape juice and turned the page. "I have learned the secret of being content in any and every situation, whether well-fed or hungry, whether living in plenty or in want. I can do everything through Him who gives me strength." The verses jumped off the page at her.

Leaning back on the pillow, she closed her eyes, and immediately Dan's words came to mind. *For we brought nothing into this world and we'll take nothing out of it.* The rest of the verse was that if we have food and clothing, we will be content with that.... It really bothered her that he could spout off a verse like that and mean it. She felt petty and ungrateful. The man had just lost everything and he might be an oaf, but he seemed like a contented one. Who flirted and kissed like he was God's gift to women.

It just wasn't right.

Keeping her eyes closed, Ashby prayed that the Lord would help her focus and be content with her own life. That she would have the fortitude to wait for the man He had for her. If she were to have babies—and oh, how she hoped she would—then she would keep her wits about her.

The coolness of the mask seeped into her as the soothing scent wrapped around her, and she prayed God would help her with the resentments that were plaguing her. She knew that without His help she was going to have trouble with all of her requests.... She took a slow breath, relaxed into the soft mattress, and somewhere along the way, fell asleep....

A knock on her front door woke Ashby. She sat straight up and blinked. The knock came again, insistently, as if it had been going for a while. Disoriented for a moment, she glanced at the clock and was shocked to find it was morning. Of course, the sunlight streaming through her window might have been a clue, if she hadn't been so distracted by the banging on her door.

She'd slept like a log, obviously; the Bible had barely moved from her lap. Closing it and pushing it into the covers, she stumbled out of bed. Who was banging on her door at seven in the morning? Clutching her robe, she yanked the door open without looking through the peephole. All grogginess disappeared when she found Dan staring back at her.

For an instant he looked startled, which was odd, given that *he'd* just knocked on *her* door. The expression disappeared quickly as a smile spread across his face. Like a floodgate opening, all the frustrations from the day before swamped Ashby...but then hope bubbled up. Maybe he'd come to apologize for his unacceptable behavior.

It was about time.

Trying to appear as if she didn't care one way or the other, she lifted her chin and met his twinkling eyes, just as she realized her skin felt tight. *Seaweed and mint mask!* Her eyes widened in dismay as she fingered the crusty remains—she could only imagine what he was seeing.

"Hello, beautiful," he crooned.

Wishing she could become the incredible shrinking woman and disappear, Ashby took one step back and, without uttering a word, slammed the door in his face. Berating herself all the way to the bathroom, she snatched up a hand towel, wetted it and started scrubbing. She could hear Dan's laughter through the door and down the hall.

She scrubbed harder as he tapped lightly on the outer door.

"Ash, open up. It's okay. I didn't mean that in a rude way."

"Go away," she shouted. Templetons didn't shout. She couldn't remember the last time she'd been mad enough to shout.

"Come on, Ash, open up. You look pretty in green."

"'You look pretty in green,'" she mimicked, then louder, for his ears, she demanded that he march back across the hallway and stay there!

He didn't. When she finally had all the green off her now bright pink face, she glared at her reflection in the mirror and knew that the only thing she could do was go answer the door. After all, four other tenants lived in the apartment house and were probably hearing everything that was going on.

Marching to the front door, she yanked it open. "What do you want?"

Smiling like Esther Mae's swashbuckling pirate, he held the plate of cheesecake toward her. "I come in peace. Stacy and the other ladies from the candy store dropped this off last night as a housewarming gift. I thought I'd share it with you."

Ashby wanted to tell him to march right back across the hallway, because she couldn't be bought. But she loved cheesecake.

And this was his peace offering.

Her stomach growled. She bit her lip as the creamy concoction called out to her.

He, in perfect pirate form, waved the plate flagrantly beneath her nose. There were three pieces, each drizzled in strawberries. The cowboy did not fight fair. Crumbling, she reached for the plate.

"Nope." He snatched it out of her reach. "You have to offer me coffee. Peace offering, remember?"

Ashby's grip on the door tightened as she gritted the top layer of enamel off her molars. The man was so sure of himself. Why couldn't he just say, "I'm sorry for acting like a jerk. Have some cheesecake. See ya later." The last thing she wanted was to spend time with him.

But he was offering an olive branch.

She stepped back to let him enter. "Have a seat," she said, indicating the bar stool in the small breakfast nook.

She stepped into the kitchen and went to work preparing her coffeemaker. She didn't have to look at him to know he was surveying her living room. The idea of him seeing her things rubbed her the wrong way. She wasn't exactly certain why, but she felt he would judge her by what he saw. If he'd thought she needed to loosen up before, there was no telling what he'd think once he took a close look at her meticulous home.

Not ready to hear his comments, she mumbled that she would be back, then hurried to her room. Let him look and judge; what did it matter what he thought of her?

Her prickliness didn't subside as she brushed her teeth, so she took extra care brushing her hair and selecting a buttercup-yellow dress for church. Finally, after she'd completed her toilette, and had no other excuse, she padded back to the kitchen.

He was lounging against the counter, studying a picture of her and her parents. He looked up when she walked into the room, and his smile took her breath away. The man could bottle that and make a mint.

The kiss immediately came to mind, and her hand shook just a little as she took two mugs off the cup stand before reaching for the pot. She'd kissed him—embarrassment surged over her. Feeling his gaze, she focused on filling the cups. "How do you take yours?" she asked, and was glad that her voice sounded normal.

"Two sugars and two creams. This you and your parents?"

"Yes," she replied, adding his sugar, then reaching

into the fridge and grabbing the cream. "They still can't believe I moved out here. I'm not certain they'll ever forgive me. Of course, if I don't give them grandchildren soon, they won't care if I never come home again."

"That bad, huh?"

She set his cup in front of him and grabbed extra plates and forks. The cheesecake lifted easily. "It's not that bad, I guess. But that's how I feel." Why was she telling him this? The last thing she needed to do was talk to him about her parents.

She focused on the cheesecake. Not the greatest breakfast in the world, but she didn't really care. She loved a good cheesecake. "This looks wonderful." She dipped her fork into her piece, then remembered herself. "We should bless this, although I'm a firm believer that God already blessed cheesecake. That's why it's so wonderful." She was proud of herself for sounding so relaxed. So at ease. Especially when her insides were churning.

Dan grinned. "I knew there was something about you that I really identified with. I could eat my weight in this stuff."

"Then bless it and let's eat." She closed her eyes for the prayer.

"Dear Lord, bless this food and the good company. Amen."

She didn't look at him as she took a bite. It was as good as she'd thought it would be. She could almost forgive him for this, she thought, as she savored the flavor and waited for him to apologize for his behavior. Of course, he'd said this was a peace offering, but that wasn't exactly an apology, at least not where she came from.

"You ran off too soon last night. You're going to have to step across the hall and see what we came up with on the decorating. Lacy enlisted the help of all the ladies from the shelter. It looks good. I think you'll like it."

Some friend Lacy was. She hadn't even come by to check on Ashby.... Then again, she would probably have been just as tickled as Esther Mae and the others.

Dan was watching her. Nothing in his expression bespoke remorse. She didn't say anything, just took a sip of coffee.

"C'mon, Ash. I know you're upset that I kissed you," he said, finally.

She set her cup down and snatched up her fork. "You're not even acting the least bit remorseful."

"That's because I'm not. I'm sorry you're upset, but it was a great kiss. Of course, if we keep practicing I could give you a few tips—"

Ashby's fork clattered to the plate. "Are you serious?"

He howled with laughter. "Ashby, come on, girl. Have a little fun. It was a kiss. And a good one at that. I was just joking about the tips—"

"You know what?" Ashby pushed her cheesecake back onto the serving plate, snatched his plate up and did the same, then handed it back to him. "Take this, go home and stay."

He looked startled, and Ashby felt a bit of satisfaction that she'd caused it. When he grinned in disbelief, she almost threw caution to the wind and tossed her coffee at him. Instead she yanked open her front door and pointed. "You are rude, obnoxious and full of yourself. Go."

He blinked, but did as she asked. Once he was in the hall, he turned back and started to say something. She slammed the door before he got a word out.

It was a very unladylike thing to do. Then again, she hadn't been feeling much like a lady as of late.

Dan was a fool. Straight up, no doubt about it. First he'd kissed Ashby yesterday and made her mad, so he'd decided after she'd stormed off that maybe the best thing was to let her calm down and give himself time to regain some semblance of control over his own emotions. Lacy and the happy matchmakers had assured him that she was probably just embarrassed by their rude behavior, not him.

He doubted that very much. She was furious with him. But she had kissed him back, and he couldn't help but feel some hope in that. He'd spent the remainder of the evening smiling on the inside. She wasn't as immune to him as she acted.

And then he'd messed up again today. He'd been so excited about that revelation that he'd let his big mouth get in his way. Talk about putting his foot in his mouth every way possible.

Staring at the door she'd slammed in his face, he berated himself for teasing her. This was one woman who didn't appreciate his sense of humor, and he couldn't seem to curb it when he was around her.

But she'd kissed him! He smiled as he went to his apartment to put the cheesecake in the refrigerator for later…because he was determined there would be a later. And when it came, he wasn't going to mess up again.

Chapter Twelve

Ashby had just parked her car in the church lot and immediately spotted Dan standing at the back of his truck talking with Emmett James, a nice cowboy, if shy. She was still seething about their earlier encounter and the fact that she'd considered throwing something. As she glanced at Dan, the feeling surged up again.

Esther Mae and Hank pulled in beside them. In her usual hurry, Esther Mae hopped out of the car, slammed the door and started toward the church at a gallop. But unknown to her, she'd caught the tail of her dress in the door, and the skirt basically yanked her feet right out from under her. Ashby was in a position to see what was happening, but it occurred so fast she didn't have time to call out a warning. Which made what happened next all the more amazing. Within the split second that it took for Esther to slam the door and start toward the ground, Dan reacted. Almost before the door snagged her dress!

One minute Esther was falling, hands and knees in serious danger of getting banged up on the white-rock parking lot, and the next instant Dan had caught her in his arms. Esther Mae barely had time to register that she was in trouble!

Riveted to the spot, Ashby watched him turn on the charm. Why, poor Esther Mae was so flustered to find herself looking up at that smile, she forgot to be shaken up about almost falling flat on her face. Ashby had to admit that Dan's aggravatingly dazzling smile had its good points.

But as she left the scene and headed toward the nursery, which she was grateful to be in charge of this morning, she wasn't exactly sure what to think of him. He made her do things she wouldn't normally even consider. Like kissing him with abandon and throwing things—that wasn't her.

That made her crazy.

Crazy wasn't good. Crazy didn't make a good foundation for any relationship. Did it?

Ashby touched her temple, where tension was building as she found herself reliving the moment. That kiss had reached inside her, and she couldn't get it off her mind. "Peter Pan syndrome," she muttered as she tugged open the doors into the church annex. She couldn't let the kiss and Dan's heroics obscure her perceptions of him. Steven had once stopped the car during a thunderstorm and rescued a puppy. That hadn't made him any less of a jerk in the end.

* * *

Dan had almost had a heart attack when he realized the door had caught the back of Esther Mae's dress. He'd always had great reflexes and they came in handy as he shot out to save her from hurting herself. Now he was doing all he could to keep her from being embarrassed.

He hadn't missed the fact that Ashby was standing to the side, watching. And he'd glanced up to find her looking at them with the most disgusted expression on her face. With no time to think about that, he righted Esther Mae and smiled, making a fuss over her.

"Thank you, Dan," she gasped, just as Hank rounded the end of the car to take her from his arms. Dan reached and grasped the door handle, and the door opened, releasing her red skirt. It had a grease spot on it now, but that was irrelevant. She could have had bleeding hands and knees, or even broken wrists if she'd reached out to break her fall.

"Honey," Hank crooned, "are you all right? That was a close one."

"I'm fine, I'm fine. Thanks to Dan. How in the world did you know I was in trouble? I felt myself start to fall when my dress yanked me back like a calf in a ropin' contest, and the next thing I know I'm in your arms!"

Dan grinned and tipped his hat to her. "I was in the right place at the right time. Any of the other cowboys would have done the same. Especially to save a lovely lady like you."

Esther blushed prettily. "They might have tried, but

that's not saying anyone would have been as quick as you. You must have moved like lightning!"

"It was beautiful," Norma Sue said, barreling up to them. She was red, too, but from hustling all the way across the parking lot. "Woo-wee! That was some fancy footwork, Dan Dawson. Esther Mae, all you needed was a pair of horns and y'all would have looked like the steer-wrestling event."

Uncomfortable with all the praise, Dan extracted himself as quickly as was polite and headed to class.

Sunday school was crowded, and he was disappointed when he realized Ashby wasn't in the room. He took a seat in the front row, where there were three vacant chairs together, and laid his Bible on the second one to hold it for her. Emmett James came in and sat down beside Dan. He and Emmett had been talking outside when Esther Mae had almost fallen. They'd been having a few conversations lately. Emmett was a quiet cowboy who wore his heart on his sleeve. Everyone knew he was in love with Stacy. Not that he'd ever told anyone that, but it was obvious. From the first moment she'd stepped off the van that had transferred her and the other residents of the women's shelter to Mule Hollow, he'd been drawn to her.

He was a shy fella, Dan's total opposite, but he had a gentle heart and a calm way about him that Dan knew Stacy had taken notice of. Emmett had worked for Clint for several years, and he was a good, godly man. Dan was rooting for him, not that Emmett had talked to Stacy much. But he hovered when she was near, and if she looked as if she needed anything, he was quick to anticipate it and get it for her. If she dropped a diaper, he'd swoop in and pick it up for her at receptions or church gatherings. If she looked thirsty, Emmett was Johnny-on-the-spot with a cup of punch or a soda. And Dan knew Stacy was not unaffected by his quiet, respectful approach.

After the mild-mannered man had confronted Dan about his intentions toward Stacy, Dan's regard for Emmett had skyrocketed. He'd eased Emmett's mind by explaining his past, something he hadn't told anyone, but felt Emmett should know. Once he learned that he and Dan had Stacy's well-being in mind, but in different ways, they'd quietly joined forces. Dan's objective was to help her learn not to be wary of men in general, which was going to benefit Emmett in the end. Emmett's objective was to win her heart, and he seemed to be a patient man. Dan knew from experience with his mom and the other women who had lived in the shelter with them when he was young that patience was exactly what Emmett was going to need.

And even that might not be enough.

Some scars ran too deep. But nothing was too large for the Lord to handle, and Dan prayed that God's healing power would touch Stacy's heart.

As he waited for Ashby to show, he and Emmett talked about the weather. When class finally got started, still without Ashby, he realized she must have nursery duty.

At least he hoped that was where she was. As angry as she was with him, she could have chosen to skip class rather than encounter him. He couldn't concentrate on what Brady was teaching for worrying over it.

She was quickly becoming an obsession with him. He couldn't get her off his mind. And that was a new experience for him.

Ashby was leaving the nursery, heading toward her car, when Dottie Cannon called to her. Lance Yates waved as she hurried across the parking lot toward where Dottie was waiting. Ashby was aware of his gaze as she reached Dottie and wondered if he'd wanted to speak with her.

"I just wanted to make sure we're still on for Friday night."

"Yes. I'm looking forward to it." The ladies from the shelter were going to a seminar in another county, and Ashby had been more than happy to agree to babysit. Max would be spending the night with a friend, so it was going to be Ashby and three darling little boys for the evening.

"I can't thank you enough. This is going to be such a good seminar."

"Are you sure five-thirty is okay?" she asked. In her peripheral vision she saw Lance climb in his truck to leave. Relief filled her as she focused on Dottie's answer.

"Yes, if we leave then, we'll have plenty of time to get there."

Ashby studied Dottie. She'd always been beautiful,

with her black hair, translucent skin and navy eyes, but Ashby thought that she'd blossomed since announcing she was three months pregnant. "Are you feeling okay?" she asked. "You look amazing."

Dottie's eyes sparkled as she smiled. "I *feel* amazing. I'm eating everything within reach, though."

Brady pulled up beside them and came around to open the door for Dottie. "I thought I'd save you a few steps." He was beaming as he placed an arm around her waist and hugged her to him. "Missed you in Sunday school, Ashby. You must have had ragamuffin duty this morning."

She laughed. "I did. Did I miss anything?"

He looked offended. "One of my excellent lessons."

Dottie leaned her head against his shoulder. "That's what I love about my man. Not a vain bone in his body."

"He's right, though, Dottie. He is a great teacher."

"I'm sure he is."

"You know," Ashby said, suddenly realizing that because Dottie taught the children's Sunday school class, she had never sat in on her husband's class, "I would love to teach in your place one morning, so that you could find out exactly what he's up to."

Dottie looked thoughtful. "I may take you up on that. When I'm further along, I might need a break."

"I'll remind you of that later on, then. Take care." She got into her car, then watched Brady help Dottie up into the seat. When he gave her a gentle kiss before closing her door and jogging around to his side, a sharp longing cut through Ashby. As she drove back toward town, she prayed that she would be so blessed, even as she hoped the best for them.

Dan had beaten her back, she saw when she pulled into the parking lot. Everyone thought she was crazy for not going out with the maddening man. And maybe she was, she admitted as she ducked into her apartment, relieved that she hadn't run into him. Yet it was the only thing she knew to do. He was dangerous to her.

Yet despite everything that had happened, she was drawn to Dan, despite his occasional bad manners.

She knew what it was. Like Steven had, Dan represented something she lacked—a carefree spirit, a missed childhood.... She halted that train of thought, refusing to let herself spiral into that shadow. Her parents couldn't help being who they were. They loved her in their own fashion. She'd been telling herself that for years, and coming to terms with it was the only way she could leave it behind. Not that she always did that. Some days were better than others. There were far worse things in this world than her silly problems. Really, sometimes she felt so petty and spoiled. Surely God thought very little of her on days like today.

Disgruntled, she changed into a white shirt and her favorite jeans. Soft and worn, they were as comfortable as a baby's jumper. Her mother would hate them, stating that they weren't fit for a lady to wear...and that was exactly why Ashby wore them.

There she went again. What was wrong with her?

She was ashamed of the idea that she wore them for

spite, but the fact was she really did love them. They didn't have any holes in them yet, but the knees were going and a couple of other places were getting threadbare, so she hand-washed them, knowing that while holes were fashionable, they also meant the end was near for her dear jeans. For a girl who'd worn frilly, fancy dresses from the moment she was born, she couldn't help that she loved dressing down. Behind closed doors only, though. Some things were too ingrained in her to completely alter. Her mother could take pride in that, at least.

She found comfort in odd places, and these jeans, worn in the comfort of her own home, were part of that.

She studied her neat, precise home. Dan had studied it, too. She'd seen the look in his eyes, but he hadn't said anything. His former home had probably been well lived-in. She'd been surprised when he hadn't said anything when she'd opened her cupboard and pulled out the canister of coffee. He probably never even thought to line his dry goods up in alphabetical order. She had no doubt that obsessing over whether each can and package faced straight ahead never entered his mind.

But then, he'd probably not lived under the microscope held up by an insecure mother.... And there Ashby went again, sliding back into places she wanted not to go.

All because of him.

She was pulling a bag of mixed vegetables from the freezer when a knock sounded on her door. She paused, her fingers tightening on the cold plastic. Despite every smart brain cell she possessed, she knew that the reckless part of her that had opted to pull her favorite jeans out of the drawer had also been hoping Dan would come knocking on her door.

Not that she knew it was him. But that was the disturbing part; she *hoped* it was him. The sane person she always tried to be, the one who focused on her dream of having children, that part of her knew this was a bad idea. But as she set the bag down and headed toward the door, she wasn't listening to that person. Not right now.

Her nerves were doing cartwheels as she ran a hand over her hair and stared at the doorknob. The knock came again. She took a deep breath and pulled the door open.

Chapter Thirteen

"Don't throw anything. I come in peace," Dan said the minute the door swung open. He almost dropped the picnic basket when he saw Ashby standing there.

Sure, he'd seen her dressed casually, but there was always a perfection to her that held people at bay. Not so in this outfit.... He let out a soft whistle, staring at her casual girl-next-door clothes and her bare feet.

This was much better than finding her with that green stuff caked on her face.

"You really know how to take a man's breath away," he said, meeting her astounding green eyes.

"You'll say anything to make up for rude behavior," she retorted, but her tone wasn't belligerent, which gave him hope.

"That's true. But the truth is you look amazing."

Her gaze wavered and she looked almost vulnerable

when she lifted her chin in that cute way she had. “In these old things…”

His insides tumbled at the uncertainty he heard in those words. Pretty as she always looked, she never seemed to believe him when he complimented her. That was part of the attraction.

But what was it about this woman that kept him coming back? It was more than that she looked amazing, he knew. Clint had told him earlier that he’d had a few of the cowboys asking if Dan and Ashby were an item. Clint hadn’t known exactly what to reply, so he had said nothing. But clearly the guys were thinking about making a move for Ashby’s affections.

One part of Dan wanted to say it was about time they stopped being stupid. It was the other part that wanted to tell them to stay away from her, that she was his. That they were an item.

Problem was, she thought he was an obnoxious flirt. The perception had never bothered him before, because he understood who he was. But he wanted Ashby to see him as more. He wanted—no, he needed her to see him. The real him. But he needed her to look deeper.

“Aren’t you going to ask me why I’m here?”

“Why *are* you here?”

He lifted the basket. “I’m trying a new tactic. I came home from church inspired to prepare this in the hopes that if you saw all the hard work and effort I went to, you wouldn’t be able to turn me down.”

“Turn you down?”

"That's right. I was hoping that once you saw how I slaved over this picnic lunch, you would feel compelled to forgive me for all my bad behavior and say yes when I asked you to go on a picnic with me."

Her gaze darted to the basket and back to him. He wiggled it for extra incentive.

She dropped her chin and leveled serious eyes at him. "What's in the hamper?"

He held it behind him. "Not telling. You only learn what's in here if you come with me."

He saw interest spark like fireflies in her emerald gaze, and could sense he had an opening. "Please don't say no." Sincerity rang in his words and he hoped she heard it. "I promise not to say anything about your alphabetized canned goods." So much for the sincerity. He hadn't meant to mention that.

Her lips twitched. "I was wondering when you were going to get around to that."

"Hey, I line my socks up in my drawers according to colors."

She chuckled. "What—white, white and more white?"

He grinned. "How did you know?"

"Good guess," she said, and he saw the tension ease out of her. "Let me get my shoes."

"Get your shoes—" he began to say, his brow creasing.

"Yes, so I can come with you."

He watched her walk down the hall, then looked up at the ceiling and mouthed a thank-you to the good Lord. He finally had a date with Ashby Templeton. *Yee-haw!*

* * *

Ashby wasn't sure what she was doing. She didn't even ask where he wanted to picnic as they climbed into his truck. He was once more the perfect gentleman, like he'd been the night he'd given her a ride after the pig scramble. He held the door for her, took her elbow as she climbed into the seat. It was a really nice feeling, and one she tried to keep in perspective. But she had to be fair, and if she was making comparisons between Dan and Steven, well, she must acknowledge that Steven had rarely held a chair for her or opened her car door for her, and on the occasions that he did, it felt like it was done as an afterthought. Not so with Dan. He made her feel special each time he gently cupped her elbow with one hand and swept the door open for her with the other. The man got points for that.

"You aren't going to ask where I'm taking you?" he asked when they were on the road.

"I thought I'd let you keep me in suspense."

He chuckled and a thrill of electricity raced through her. Ashby inhaled at the shock and tried to tell herself she wasn't a fool.

"I like you, Ash. You're one cool cucumber."

"I'm not so certain a girl wants to be called a cool cucumber. Especially from a guy who insists she needs to loosen up."

Dan's eyes were serious when they met hers. "Sorry about that. I was way out of line."

"No big deal. I know it better than anyone."

"I don't think so. I've been known to be wrong." He glanced again at her. "Honestly."

"Say it isn't so," she gasped, slapping a hand over her heart the way she'd seen him do so many times.

He grinned. "Look, I still don't know what happened the day of that bike race." The expression on his face made it clear he wondered whether the disgruntled woman he'd met that day could reemerge. "But I'm thinking we have both misjudged each other in a lot of ways."

"You might be right," she said, her voice soft.

He held out a hand toward her. "Hi, I'm Dan Dawson, and I'd like to start over."

He wanted things to change between them. And if he had his way, things were changing starting today.

She didn't immediately take his hand, and he was forced to glance back at the road. But he stubbornly kept his hand extended, fingers stretching toward her. When she firmly slipped her slender hand into his he had the sudden urge to slam on the brakes so he could jump out and run a few victory laps around the truck.

Instead he squeezed her hand and smiled. "You have just made my day."

"Somehow I can't bring myself to believe that. Though we may have misjudged each other a little."

"A little?" he teased. "You think all I do is flirt, and I—" He stopped abruptly, thinking maybe he'd better not go there.

She laughed again. "You do flirt a lot." She removed her hand when he looked at her with a frown. "And you kissed me out of the blue. I still don't get that."

He looked at her lips. *He* got it. And now he was about to shoot himself in the foot, so he hoped honesty would pay off. "What can I say? You just looked so kissable."

She rolled her eyes. "Does that line actually work for you?"

Her question dug deep. "It wasn't a line." It had been the absolute truth. She looked at him with eyes that said she wasn't sure if she trusted his words. "Ashby, contrary to what you think, I don't normally kiss women out of the blue, as you put it." His driveway came into view and he focused on his place instead of the bale of hay that was suddenly lodged in his throat.

Someone had delivered the dozer since he'd left yesterday. It sat waiting for the crew to continue working tomorrow.

"So they level it tomorrow," Ashby said, all humor gone as she effectively changed the subject.

"Looks that way. I'll be glad when they finish. I'm thinking positively about it, but the ruins aren't the most pleasant thing to see every day." He hadn't said that to anyone.

"You really have a great outlook on the whole situation. You inspired me...and surprised me."

Ashby's soft words startled him and bolstered him at the same time. Maybe she didn't think he was a complete loss. "Thank you," he said, meeting her smile with one of his own.

"I just thought since we were turning over a new leaf, so to speak, that I should be honest with you."

As he drove on past the house, following the gravel road that weaved through his pastures, Dan suddenly felt much better. He and Ashby were turning over a new leaf—sounded good to him. Real good.

"So you think there is some hope for the incorrigible Mr. Dawson?"

She laughed. "Maybe. But don't get a big head."

"Who, me? Never." He pulled the truck to a stop beneath a giant oak. "Besides, I know the only reason you're being so nice to me is because you think I have the other half of that cheesecake in the basket."

"And you would be absolutely right."

An irresistible pull of attraction connected them as their eyes met and held.

Ashby's defenses were crumbling around her when it came to Dan and she knew it.

"Where are we?" she asked, tearing her attention away.

"That is a surprise," he said.

Ashby didn't look at him, but could hear the smile in his voice, and even that did weird things to her insides. She hopped out of the truck before he made it around to open her door for her. Her mother's frown would have been huge—which made Ashby smile.

"Can I get in on the secret?" Dan said, taking the picnic basket from the back seat.

Embarrassment scorched her cheeks and she kicked a stone, feeling foolish. And slightly mean. "I'm ashamed to say it was me behaving badly."

"Now, I thought we were over that?"

She laughed. "My mother's voice follows me around sometimes. She would really hate that I got out of the truck without allowing you to open the door for me."

"Ahh, and my mother would have had my ear for not moving faster to get it open."

Ashby bit her lip to hold back a goofy grin. "Mothers."

Now it was his turn to laugh. "Gotta love 'em. This way." He started walking ahead of her. "Watch your step."

She followed him along a rocky path that wound past a large prickly pear cactus covered with huge yellow blooms. It was beautiful in its unique way. "So where are we going?" she asked, looking down, watching her footing.

"Here, just over this hill." He took her arm and helped her step around a large rock. His hand remained under her elbow as they topped the ridge, and she welcomed the protectiveness. And the feel of it, too.

"Oh!" She gasped at the field of sunflowers spread out before her. They were amazing, their large faces lifted to the sun. "What a happy place," she said, unable to take her eyes off the sea of yellow backed by the clear blue sky.

"Exactly what I hoped you would think," Dan said softly.

"Did you plant these?"

"Nope. Just happened upon them one day when I was riding."

Ashby needed to pinch herself. She really did. How in the world had she ended up on a sunny Sunday afternoon, standing in a sunflower patch with a drop-dead-gorgeous cowboy?

"You're doing that smile thing again, where your eyes seem filled with secrets of their own. Tell me you're not thinking of your mother again. I gotta admit it doesn't do a cowboy's ego any favors when his date keeps thinking of her mother." Dan pushed his hat back and gave her his Harry Connick Jr. smile.

"No, I'm not thinking of my mother. Anybody ever tell you that you look like Harry Connick Jr.?"

He handed her the basket, then pulled the blanket from his shoulder. "I was really hoping you'd love me for me. Not that I have anything against the guy. But I am better-looking. I was thinking more like that other guy, you know—*People Magazine*'s sexiest man alive."

Ashby laughed. "Oh, please, don't let me hurt your ego."

"You're not." He winked at her, then spread the blanket on the ground . They sat down with the basket between them.

"While I pull out this mighty fine feast that I've prepared for you, tell me about yourself. Consider it the tax."

Ashby folded her hands in her lap and watched him peek inside the basket with a mischievous glint in his eyes. "I know you came here from somewhere in California," he continued. "This town is growing with a ton of people from out there. What's up with that?"

It was true. "Isn't that the oddest thing? I'd say it has to do with the original ad campaign that the local ladies started when they advertised for wives. I think they targeted the West Coast and a few Southern states. Dottie and the ladies from the shelter didn't come here because of the ad, though."

"Nope, God led them here. Don't you think?"

Ashby studied Dan. For a man, he seemed so sure about that. Not that a guy couldn't sound sincere about the mysteries of the way God worked, but Dan accepted it with such ease. "Yes, I do believe He did. I believe we each eventually end up where God wants us, but that He can use us wherever we are."

"Yup. That's another way to look at it. Either way, I believe God's in control."

As if Ashby was a student being rewarded for giving the right answer, Dan pulled out a plate of cheesecake, his grin widening when she wilted with happiness.

Ashby watched Dan pull out the food—thick roast beef sandwiches, a couple of bottles of water and a bowl of strawberries. Her stomach growled in a very unladylike fashion as he set the food in front of her on the blanket.

"Whoa, the lady is hungry," he teased, handing her a sandwich. When she went to take it from him, he held on, grinning. "Let's thank the good Lord for that cheesecake."

Ashby was embarrassed to realize she hadn't bowed

her head along with him. She was too stunned, too amazed by this day. What an unlikely turnaround just a few short hours could make. As he prayed, she found herself studying the way his dark hair fell across his forehead and how long his dark lashes were against his skin. She didn't mean to be distracted, but she got caught up before she knew what hit her. This man was such a contradiction.

When he finished his blessing, he lifted his eyes to hers. The look she saw there was as warm as the sunlight, and sent her heart skipping. Dangerous stuff. Glancing away, she hoped he couldn't see the confusion she was feeling.

"So tell me about your family," he said.

"My family?"

He nodded. "Yeah, do you have a big family or a little one? I want to know the nitty-gritty on Ashby Templeton. Although, if you want, you can tell me to mind my own business."

Ashby hesitated. She was grateful to have something to focus on other than the way he made her feel, but talking about her family wasn't her first choice. Dan was watching her closely, and she gave him a weak smile. "They live in Pacific Heights. I'm an only child." Her words sounded jerky even to her own ears, and she realized talking about her parents wasn't going to be easy. What had she been thinking? She took a bite of the sandwich and tried desperately to relax.

People talked about family. It was normal conversation. Especially on first dates. It was supposed to be a safe topic.

Dan watched Ashby with open interest. She looked like she was sitting in a five-star restaurant instead of on a blanket in the middle of a sunflower patch. He couldn't stop the smile watching her evoked. "Were they supportive of your move?"

She shook her head, swallowing before she elaborated. "No. Not at all. I can't blame them, though. If I'm ever lucky enough to have children, I'll hate to see them move away from me. I'll want to cling to them and never let them go." She sighed. "I only hope I have children who can tolerate me. I feel for them already."

Ashby's gaze avoided him as she took another bite of her sandwich, a very small bite off the corner. Something was up between her and her parents. He heard it in her voice and saw it in her eyes when she spoke of them. She was trying hard to hide it, but it was there. He knew how to read between the lines when it came to what people said about their families.

He changed the subject, not wanting to upset her, despite his burning curiosity. But he couldn't help digging deeper into her other statement. Even though it might be a bit personal for a first date, for him it was of major importance. "So how badly do you want children?"

Her eyes grew wistful. "With all my heart. I dream of them."

Dan swallowed hard, caught off guard by her sweetness. Ashby would be a gentle and caring mother.

"Do you want children?"

He blinked, her words slapping him out of his brain freeze. "I haven't decided yet," he blurted out, sounding like a bumbling idiot. He cleared his throat, hoping to clear the fog out of his brain. "I've got a lot to get done before I think about it, though. I do have long-term plans, despite what you may think." That hadn't come out right.

She sat straighter, as if he'd just irritated her with his jibe.

She put her sandwich down. "I never said you didn't have long-term plans."

"I heard differently. Besides, what were you to expect? It's not like I act as if I do," he said more gently, hoping to ease the moment, knowing it was the truth. He wanted her to see him in a better light, yet he kept saying things the wrong way.

She shifted. "Well, like we already agreed, maybe we've both jumped to conclusions about each other that were incorrect."

She had him there. "We did say that, didn't we?"

The air crackled as she lifted an eyebrow, giving him her best "so there" look. At least that's what he thought it was. He chuckled. He liked Ashby Templeton. And was more than a little curious about what secrets lay behind her beautiful eyes.

"How about that cheesecake?" he asked, passing her the whole plate.

Those mysterious eyes sparkled as she took it. "Do your peace offerings always work?"

Feeling great, he gave her a teasing smirk, stretched out on the blanket, crossed his boots, then folded his hands behind his head and studied the clouds. "As long as I use cheesecake."

"Have I told you lately that you are incorrigible?"

"Yup," he said, still grinning. "But you can again. I really like the way you say it."

Chapter Fourteen

"I noticed he always seeks Stacy out," Ashby said on Thursday, as she and Rose were putting out new merchandise. She couldn't help herself; she had a great need to have certain questions about Dan answered. Rose lived at the shelter and might be able to give her some insight into the man she'd begun to think about on a constant basis since their Sunday picnic. Not that she'd seen him since then. He might be her neighbor, but he worked such long hours, what with all the jobs he did, that she hadn't seen hide nor hair of him all week.

Seriously, since he was a part-time farrier, she'd contemplated buying a horse that needed shoes just so she could hire him.

Something had happened out there in his sunflower field, and her mind had returned over and over to the two-hour lunch spent there with Dan. Some would say it was a romantic experience.... She found herself having to push that picture out of her mind. It had been an eye-opening experience. She had very much enjoyed his company. They'd talked and laughed, and she'd been sad when he'd finally taken her home. If anything, it'd given her more food for thought. Particularly regarding the things that baffled and worried her about him.

Rose met her questioning gaze with a smile. "He's a dear that way. Do you know he's one of the shelter's biggest donors? I'm not supposed to know that, but I was in the office one day when Dottie was doing the books, and I saw the ledger. I should feel bad about snooping, but I don't. It really made my respect for him escalate."

Ashby was stunned twice over. First, over the fact that Dan did this on a regular basis, and second, that Rose would tell her something that was surely supposed to be confidential. Rose was not a gossip.

As if reading her thoughts, her friend blushed. "I know I shouldn't have said that, but I thought you might need to know."

"Why would I need to know that?" Ashby asked, placing an aquamarine dress on a hanger. Walking to the far wall, she hung it on the end of a display. She fiddled and fluffed, feeling Rose's scrutiny.

"Ashby, I work with you. Plus, remember our talk at Max's birthday party? Come on, it's no secret that you've seriously got a problem with something about him. And I don't know that there's any real cause for that."

Ashby glanced over her shoulder and nodded. "I

have to admit that I may have misjudged him a little." Not that she knew all that much about him. Somehow, on Sunday he'd managed to keep the conversation away from himself. At least, away from anything personal. She wasn't sure how it had happened, but she'd realized later that he'd skillfully avoided telling her much that she didn't already know.

All she'd learned about him was that he hadn't decided if he wanted children. Since she wasn't planning on marrying him, this information shouldn't have bothered her. But it did. Personally, she couldn't understand how anyone would consider not having children. And given how much fun he'd seemed to have with the boys at Max's birthday party, it was a surprise that he felt that way. It made her curious about him, and as much as she hated admitting it, there was a spot in her heart that felt sorry.

She would never marry a man who didn't want children. But she would never marry Dan Dawson anyway, so what did that matter?

Still, her defenses around him had crumbled despite her reservations, but nothing else had changed. "He flirts so much, though. With everyone, especially Stacy, and she is very fragile. Doesn't that seem like he's toying with her?" Ashby just couldn't shake that thought.

Rose looked thoughtful. "Like I told you, pay attention to the way he talks to Stacy, or any of the gals from the shelter. You'll realize there's a difference in the way he flirts with you." She grinned when Ashby frowned.

"It's true. He teases us like he would sisters. That's not what he does when he's talking to you. And I'm telling you, his eyes light up when he looks at you."

"You had me there for a moment. But his eyes do not light up. Even if they did, the man has said he isn't interested in a serious relationship. He doesn't even know if he wants children."

"He'll want children when he meets the right mother for them." Rose propped her hands on her hips. "And if you polled a hundred married men, I bet most would say they felt the very same way up until the day they met their wives. Ashby, take a chance and see where things go. If there were any spark between me and Dan you can be sure I wouldn't be twiddling my thumbs. That is a good man. And I love that playful side of him."

Ashby bit her lip, thinking about how much she'd enjoyed his company and how much she'd hoped to see him all week. If she was honest with herself, she had to admit she'd been disappointed that their paths hadn't crossed. "I did enjoy our lunch together." And there was the kiss, she thought, though she didn't say anything about it to Rose. There had also been a moment as he'd left her at her door… She'd thought he might kiss her again, so she'd thanked him for a lovely time and hurried inside before he'd had a chance. "Still, I don't think so," she hedged, biting her lip.

"What? Ashby, if he asks you out again, go. You can't know if there is real chemistry there unless you spend time together. Right?"

Right, Ashby thought. But that was the problem: she knew there *was* chemistry between them. And it scared her more than anything had in a very long time.

Dan had a busy week. Between buying cattle for several clients, and his farrier business, he sometimes didn't have time to tend to his own ranch. He would put his blacksmith hat on next week and shoe a few horses, but this week had been all about buying cattle. As he turned off the interstate and headed toward Mule Hollow on Friday afternoon, he was glad to be home.

When he pulled into his driveway to drop off his cattle trailer, he had mixed emotions looking at the newly cleaned foundation slab. But he refused to let himself dwell on it, and was glad Will had the final draft of the plans for the new house ready for him to pick up.

It was almost four o'clock as he drove over. Dan couldn't help but admire Will's yard. He and his wife, Haley, spent hours working there. It was nice the way they loved spending time together. Dan wondered if they knew how lucky they were to have each other. What it would mean to their children to grow up in the stable environment they were building for them.

He rang the doorbell and within seconds the heavy, custom-made door was pulled open by Haley. Tall, with a mass of blond curls, Haley Sutton looked like one of those Barbie dolls. She was a knockout and as sweet as they came. She was also a smart businesswoman who'd recently opened a real estate office on Main Street.

"Dan." She laughed, and he could hear grumbling coming from down the hall behind her. "Hurry! Get in here and settle this debate we're having." She snagged his arm and tugged him into the house. Dan was laughing, too, as she practically dragged him into the back den.

Will was standing in the middle of the room. "Hey, buddy," he called over his shoulder. "If I were you I'd grab the plans and run." He nodded toward the table where a cylinder lay. Dan assumed his blueprints were inside it.

"No," Haley said, crossing to stand beside her husband and wrapping an arm around his waist when he draped his arm across her shoulders. "Dan, you have to tell us which you prefer—Dusty Tan or Hazy Hummus?"

"Hazy Hummus?" Dan echoed. "What kind of a name is that?" He and Will looked at each other and laughed.

"Don't laugh, I didn't name it that." Haley scrunched up her nose.

"Please tell her we can't have a room painted Hazy Hummus," Will pleaded, covering her mouth with his palm when she started to protest. "It's just not right. Dusty Tan is a cowboy color, while Hazy Hummus sounds like something rolled over and died in the garden." Haley was trying to speak past Will's hand, her eyes sparkling with mirth.

Dan grinned, watching them. "Sounds like some of the green stuff that grows in my refrigerator. Hazy Hummus is the paint sample on the left?"

Will was nodding violently, but couldn't speak, since Haley had twisted around and covered *his* mouth with her own hand, all the time giggling too hard to answer. They were acting like kids! And far too absorbed in their playful debate to really care what his opinion was. It was plenty obvious to Dan that he'd interrupted what promised to be an enjoyable argument.

He stepped to the side table and picked up the cylinder. It was more than clear three was a crowd. "I think y'all can figure this out on your own. Although," he said, pausing at the hallway, "I'd go with the tan. Guys have to draw the line somewhere, and penicillin on the wall—not good. Thanks for these. Talk to ya tomorrow."

"Yeah, I'll phone you," Will called after him. But Dan noticed he didn't try to stop him from leaving.

Marriage. Some folks had a way of making it look mighty appealing.

Dan grinned as he closed the door and strode toward his truck. One day, when he was ready and the time was right, he was going to have what those two had.

And as she had off and on all week, Ashby Templeton moved out of the shadows of his thoughts and took over again. There was no denying that he'd enjoyed their Sunday-afternoon picnic. She was a puzzle he'd been toying with ever since they'd parted at her door that afternoon.

He'd left with a load of cattle early the next morning, and hadn't gotten in until late. It had been that way every day this week. He'd thought a couple of times about knocking on her door, but figured she probably wouldn't be too excited to have her crazy neighbor waking her up at almost midnight. Especially if he didn't have cheesecake. Tonight, he was arriving at a decent hour and he hoped she was home.

Chapter Fifteen

She was late. She was late. She was late. Ashby hurried down the stairs, intent on getting to the shelter. Out of necessity, she'd taken time to change from the dress she'd worn to the store today into a pair of slacks. Anticipating a lively night of crawling around on the floor, playing with a herd of rambunctious little boys, she'd thought it only prudent. Still, she hated that she was running late. A flat tire was not what she needed to find waiting for her in the parking lot.

"Not now," she groaned, just as Dan pulled into the parking lot.

"Hey," she called, before he'd barely come to a stop. "I have a flat and need a ride. Quick." Without waiting for an invitation, she wrenched open the door and hopped in.

"Sure," he said, putting the truck in Reverse and backing out without even hesitating. At the road he paused. "Where are we going?"

"No Place Like Home. I'm babysitting the boys while everyone goes to a meeting, and I'm supposed to be there in five minutes."

He grinned at her. "And so you shall be."

As he headed the truck in the right direction, she put on her seat belt. "Thank you for this. I hate to make the ladies get off to a late start, since they have a two-hour drive ahead of them."

"No problem. So, are you going to have any help?"

She glanced at him, and though she really hated to admit it, she was happy to see him. "Nope. Just me and the boys. The little boys. Max went home after school with a friend."

"Aren't you the brave one."

She met his smile with one of her own. "Not really. They're good little dudes. And contrary to rumors circulating around town, I can hang with the best of them when it comes to playing."

He laughed. "You're never going to let me live that down, are you?"

"After the hard time you gave me? Not on your life, cowboy."

When they got to the shelter, there was a flurry of action as last-minute details were shared and Dottie and the four other ladies piled into the van and drove away.

Dan was standing on the porch conversing with the three toddlers when Ashby turned back from waving goodbye.

"The boys and I thought the swings might be fun," he said, grinning like a kid himself.

Ashby's heart did a little happy skipping of its own as she looked at the motley entourage. It was a very dangerous picture. "I thought you'd be heading back to town."

"Dan, play wiff us," Jack said, tugging on his hand.

Dan grinned at Ashby. "Only if you make me. Why should these guys get to hang with the prettiest gal in the county while I have to go home alone?"

"You come swing," Gavin said, joining his brother. The twins looked nothing alike, but they obviously thought alike.

"Wait, little buddy, we have to see what the boss says." Dan lifted an eyebrow and gave Ashby that smile.

Looking at the smiling man, Ashby couldn't imagine him saying he might not want kids. He was a natural with them. "Okay. You can swing with us." Somehow this evening had taken an unexpected turn down an avenue she wasn't so sure she was going to be able to navigate intelligently.

"Yee-haw, boys, it's a go!" Dan whooped and swung baby Bryce into his arms as Gavin and Jack raced down the steps. In a flash the boys rounded the corner to the huge swing set the men from town had built.

Dan held his arm out to her. "Going my way?"

Rose's words from the day before rang in Ashby's head. Was there a difference in the way he flirted with her? Or the way he looked at her?

She hated to admit it, but she hoped so because, call

her a fool, the man had a way of looking at her that completely took her breath away.

Her brains, too, for that matter.

"How'd the twain go 'gin?" Jack asked, then yawned.

He was the last holdout from falling asleep, and Dan stood in the doorway and watched as Ashby stroked the boy's bangs out of his heavy-lidded eyes.

"Toot-toot," she answered.

From his position, Dan couldn't see her face, but he could hear the smile in her voice.

He yawned himself as she continued the story she'd been telling the twins. Gavin had faded moments before, and Dan knew it was only a matter of minutes before Jack gave up the fight.

All night Dan had been acutely aware of how good Ashby was with the boys. The three-year-olds were extremely curious and seemed to be very well adjusted. And they were happy. Their mothers had done well getting them away from their violent fathers at such a young age. Unlike him, these boys would probably have no memories of their past life...which was a good thing. His mother had lived with the regret that she'd kept him in harm's way until he was six. He sometimes thought that one reason he'd been so quick to start smiling once he was in the shelter was that he'd been so grateful he hadn't gotten a beating that day.

"Dan, are you awake?"

Ashby's soft whisper in his ear startled him. He

opened his eyes. “Sure I am. I was just thinking,” he said, pushing the thoughts away. He didn’t let himself think of those first years of his life often. Someday, hopefully, they’d ebb from his memories completely. But since that wasn’t happening, he usually shut them down on his own when they tried to rise to the surface. Looking at Ashby, he felt a longing deep inside him. She would make a wonderful mother. She made him long for a family.

“Come on, let’s get going so we don’t wake anyone up.” He draped his arm over Ashby’s shoulders and hugged her gently as they walked downstairs together. “I’m worn-out. Who’d ’a thought three dudes barely to my knees had that much energy?”

Ashby chuckled. “But isn’t it wonderful?”

“Yep.”

When they got to the living room, he dropped onto the couch and plopped his sock feet on the coffee table. He’d had a blast, but he was looking forward to a little alone time with the head babysitter. He patted the cushion beside him. “Come on down here, darlin’, and put your pretty feet up here beside mine. You earned it.”

She hesitated, then made his day when she took the seat beside him. He didn’t put his arm around her, but leaned so that their shoulders were touching. He yawned again.

“Hey, cowboy, you really sound tired.”

“It has been a long week.” He closed his eyes.

“I noticed you weren’t around much.”

He yawned again. “Been up since four this morning.”

"No wonder you're yawning. It's after nine now."

"Yep," he said, his eyes still closed. "Tell me again how the train goes."

Ashby chuckled softly and he felt her gentle fingers brush his hair off his forehead. "Toot-toot," she said, and continued to gently stroke his hair with her fingers.

Dan sighed contently and fell asleep.

"Good morning, ladies," Dan said, entering the candy store. Nive and Lynn always worked the front counter of the shop, while Stacy was more comfortable staying in the back, making the goodies he so loved to eat. Because she wasn't at ease interacting with customers, he always walked to the end of the counter to where he could see through the swinging saloon doors and made it a point to include her. "Hey, Stacy. You making something delicious back there?"

"Truffles," she said, her doe eyes darting to his before returning to the chocolate mixture she was working with.

"That's what I'm talking about!" he said with gusto, winning a chuckle from all of them, including Stacy. Which made him smile. "Anybody ever tell you girls that you have some busy boys? Man, they wore me down last night."

"Tell us something we don't know," Lynn said. "Esther Mae and Norma Sue are watching them right now, though, and believe it or not, it'll be the boys who'll be worn out by the time we get home."

"That was nice of you to help Ashby last night," Nive said. "She really loves babies."

Dan nodded. "I could tell. She didn't actually need me, of course. The woman had it under control."

"She has excellent maternal instincts," Lynn said.

That was for certain. She'd been so good with the boys. And then he'd fallen asleep. When she woke him up at eleven and told him the van was pulling up outside, she'd already cleaned up the disaster the boys had made in the living room and had the kitchen cleaned up, too.

She'd been working while he'd been sleeping. It hadn't been exactly the scenario he'd envisioned when he'd sat down on the couch.

"Speaking of mothers," he said, getting back to the reason for his trip to the candy store. "Stacy, you'll never guess what I saw this week when I was down in the back section of my property, checking cows."

She paused in her mixing and looked across the space between them. "What?" Her voice was as soft as a breath of air.

"A mama raccoon and four babies balancing on a wire fence."

"Balancing," all three ladies echoed.

He chuckled. "Yeah, they were hanging on with both front and back feet. If they'd been opossums they'd have been using their tails, too."

Stacy smiled. "You're teasing. Raccoons can't do that, can they?"

"Now you hurt my feelings," he joked, looking crestfallen when she glanced at him again. "I don't need to tease about something that's true. Maybe they were raccoons that had been raised by an opossum, and they were trying to blend in. That's my story and I'm sticking to it."

She giggled, and it was like the sweet, clear sound of a wind chime. "D-did they run?"

"Yep." He relaxed against the counter and winked at Nive, who was watching him with knowing eyes. She winked before going back to filling what looked like a big order. The candy store supplied specialty shops in several surrounding towns, and kept the ladies busy. Dan watched Stacy wipe her hands on a cloth, then move the pan to the cooling rack.

"So, I saw Emmett the other day," he said, eliciting a new blush. "He told me he's buying a house."

She walked from the back, tugging off the net that held her long hair out of her face. "Dottie told me," she said, stopping a few steps away and running her hand along the counter edge. She looked up at him. "He did, too."

Dan grinned. "Talked to ya, did he?" He'd told Emmett he needed to start talking to her instead of just hovering.

Her lips curved and her eyes dropped again as she nodded. "He's quiet."

Dan wanted to burst out laughing. Emmett was so quiet the two of them could have a date in a library. Instead of saying that Dan just grinned. "He's a good man," he said. "He's the kind of man a woman could trust."

She bit her lip and a pained expression crept into her eyes as she studied the street through the window. "I know."

The words were almost a whisper. Dan knew she knew it, but it would take more than that for her heart to convince her head that she could trust him. And that was something Dan couldn't fix for her. He could only build a friendship and a bridge of trust that might extend to others.

"Hey, I'm thinking about having a barbecue out at my place since the site is all cleaned up. What do you think about that? You know, to thank everyone for all their help." The idea had hit him on the spur of the moment, but he found he liked it, for several reasons. Asking Stacy's advice might build her confidence, he did need to thank everyone for all they'd done and a party meant Emmett and Stacy would have an opportunity to socialize.

Dan thought of Ashby and liked the idea of socializing a little himself.

"That would be nice."

"Would you come?"

Stacy looked down.

"Emmett will be there." He was pushing, he knew, but a man needed to push when things were going his way. She nodded. "Then it's a done deal. Hey, ladies," he called to Nive and Lynn. "We're having a party."

Chapter Sixteen

Ashby hadn't been home from work long before she heard a knock on her door. When she looked through the peephole and saw Dan, her heart leaped in her chest. She'd thought of him all day, but was surprised to have such a strong reaction. That startled her as much as seeing him holding a handful of huge sunflowers.

"I saw these earlier and thought of you," he said when she'd pulled the door open. He was smiling, but the minute their eyes met his smile disappeared.

"They're beautiful. Is something wrong?" she asked as she took the flowers.

"Do you have a few minutes?" He lifted the cylinder in his other hand.

"Sure. Are they the plans for your house?"

"Yup." He followed her inside, and while she got a vase out of the cabinet, he removed the lid and let the contents slide out onto her table.

Despite her own unruly feelings, she was curious about what he'd come up with. She situated the flowers in the vase, then hurried over to study the drawings, telling herself that she had things under control. She was not falling for this cowboy.

The blueprints were for a nice-size four bedroom with an open floor plan. "I like the flow," she said, pointing from the kitchen to the den and adjoining dining area. She and Dan were standing close and she was distracted by the scent of fresh soap and aftershave.

He swallowed and his gaze drifted to her lips. Just as quickly they shot back to the plans. "For some reason I thought you'd go for a formal setting. With the way your house is—" he cleared his throat "—so neat."

She stared at him, unreasonably insulted by the remark. "Just because I like a neat house doesn't mean I'm formal. Not that there's anything wrong with that." She thought of the rather stately living room and huge formal dining room in the home she'd grown up in. "My mother likes a very neat house and she runs a tight ship, as the saying goes. Anyway, neat isn't a bad thing." *Obsessive is, though.*

"I didn't mean that as an insult. To each their own."

Ashby didn't believe him. She studied her small apartment with a critical eye. "I prefer something a bit more relaxed than my mother's preference. A little more child-friendly.... I guess you couldn't tell that by looking, though." She suddenly wanted to run about and shake things up, throw a couple of pillows on the floor.... He was completely right in his assumptions. He could only judge her by what he saw of her actions and in her surroundings.

He gently cupped her chin and turned her to look at him. It was almost as if he could read her thoughts. "Like I said, I didn't say it was a bad thing. Kids will help you relax. You'll be a great mother, Ash. I saw that the other night. You were like supermama."

His hand slid from her chin to the side of her neck. She was certain that he could feel her pulse racing.

She tried to remind herself not to react this way with him. She reminded herself that she'd watched him go into the candy store earlier. She'd been surprised to see him and had hoped he would drop by her shop to say hello, but he hadn't. She'd peered through the window when, a few minutes later, he'd exited the store whistling, gotten into his truck and driven off. Once again, she'd been left feeling like one of his many flirtations. That he'd helped her babysit didn't mean anything.

And he'd looked so happy leaving the candy store. Could Rose be wrong? Could Dan really have feelings for Stacy? That could be why he donated so much money to the shelter.

Looking at him now, savoring his touch, Ashby felt an ache deep inside her chest. She swung toward the table and blinked as the plans there blurred. Oh, no, she wasn't. She refused to feel sorry for herself, and the last person she wanted seeing her tear up was Dan. If he was truly drawn to Stacy, then Ashby should be happy for the woman, who definitely deserved happiness. And Dan really seemed to be a caring man beneath his flirtatiousness. Rose had been right when she'd said he was playful. And he *was* a good man…

He was standing so close! He hadn't said anything, but she could feel him watching her. Needing distance to get her head on straight, she went to the refrigerator. Her movements were jerky as she opened the door and pulled out a pitcher of iced tea.

The truth was, after talking with Rose, and then playing with Dan and the toddlers last night, Ashby had all but decided to take a step out on faith. To see if this connection she felt with Dan really meant anything… *Stupid. Silly. Dangerous.* Especially since she knew children weren't a certainty in his future.

"Ash, are you all right?" He'd followed her.

She willed her voice to behave. "I'm fine." But she wasn't and she knew it.

Dan had to wonder what he was doing here, standing in Ashby's kitchen wanting nothing more than to kiss her sweet lips.

He'd come to town earlier to see her, and had forced himself to detour to the candy store instead. After the wonderful time they'd had taking care of the kids, something had changed. And he'd realized he didn't exactly know what was going on in his head. So he'd taken the safe route, gone to see Stacy and the others instead.

But he'd thought about Ashby all day long, and

after checking the cows at his place he hadn't been able to resist cutting her a handful of sunflowers and swinging by.

Yep, he was one messed-up pooch.

Standing this close, he was having a hard time maintaining his composure. He took a step closer still, until they were almost touching. These irrational feelings were new to him.

She drew a shuddering breath, then slid away from him and snatched up the tea pitcher out of the refrigerator. "So, when are they going to start construction?" she asked, her voice betraying her breathlessness.

Fighting not to reach for her, Dan watched her pour tea into glasses. He wondered if she realized she hadn't asked him if he wanted any. She was shaken, all right. As shaken as he was.

Again, the worry that had dogged him all week hit him like a wrecking ball. "In a couple of weeks," he said, focusing on her question. "The contractor I'm using is finishing up a couple of other projects before he can get started on mine. That means you're going to have to put up with me as a neighbor for a while." He tried to make his voice light.

Placing the tea glasses on the table, she sat down and studied the plans. Drawn to her, he sat down beside her, close enough to catch the sweet scent of her hair. He inhaled deeply, leaning closer to her.

"I-I've noticed you seem to seek out Stacy all the time," Ashby said, her eyes darting to his, then away.

Not exactly the conversation he'd been expecting. Her words distracted him from studying how graceful the curve of her neck was from her earlobe down to her shoulder.

Pulling back, he focused on her words. "I love it when Stacy talks," he said, proud of the headway Stacy had made. "Not that she says a whole lot. But we're making progress. With someone who has suffered what she has, patience, persistence and love are the key to getting her to come out of her shell. It does my heart good to see it happening." He was startled by how neat it felt to share that with Ashby.

Her green eyes filled with compassion. "You really care for her, don't you?"

He cared. "Yeah, I do." He rolled the glass between his palms and watched the ice bob as he made a decision. "I know firsthand what she's going through. My—" He cleared his throat as it threatened to close off. But he wanted to share this with Ashby. "I lived at a shelter for almost two years, starting when I was six. And even after we got our own place, we volunteered at the shelter. So we remained connected to the women and other kids coming through the shelter."

There were only three people who knew his background: Emmett, Brady and Dottie. Ashby was reacting as he'd suspected she would—with great empathy. He felt comfortable revealing his past to her. He'd been afraid he'd see pity, but that wasn't the case at all.

"I'm glad the shelter was there for you," she said.

"Your mother must have been a remarkable woman." She blinked hard.

"She was." He took a deep breath, feeling the familiar ache when he thought of her.

"Tell me about her."

He smiled. "She was very much like Stacy. She was a timid woman. I never heard her say a harsh word. Her voice was soft...." Even when things were at their worst, the quietness of her voice remained more vivid to him than the rage in his father's. "She hadn't wanted me to remember the anger, or the blows. It took more guts than I can even begin to imagine, and more love for me, for her to escape to the shelter. Violence is often handed down from father to son, if the cycle isn't broken early enough. My mother feared for my life and the lives of my children, if I lived to have any."

Tears welled in Ashby's eyes. "I can't bear to think about it. And you and your mother lived it."

"She always said loving me gave her the strength to trust that the Lord would take care of us. That He was in control, and she just had to choose the path we were to follow. I look at Stacy and Rose and the others and see her."

"Why would you let me think such horrible things about you?" Ashby asked him, anger flaring in her voice.

His throat felt as tight as his chest. He took a swallow of tea. She waited, watching him. Dan had never tried to explain it before. He rammed a hand through his hair.

"Why?" she asked again, the anger dissipating somewhat.

He realized he wanted to share his past with Ashby. "My mother taught me to minister to others. I used to love to make her smile. I found out early that I had a knack for teasing a smile out of her. I soon learned I could do it with the other ladies at the shelter."

Ashby laid a soft hand on his arm. Her touch warmed him instantly and he met her gaze.

"I can just see you as a little boy. You learned to flirt early, didn't you?" The look in her eyes made his heart melt.

"Yeah. I did."

He told her how he'd soon become the shelter's resident clown. And how he would go with his mother later on to help minister to the families that came after them. He'd learned a slow, easy smile and a kind word didn't always get him a smile in return; he had to keep going back, and pushing for that smile. "Winning the ladies' trust was all-important to me."

He stopped talking, aware that Ashby's hand still rested on his forearm. It was a simple touch, but he was amazed at how comfortable he felt with her. Looking at her, he'd never felt so connected to anyone.

Gazing at Dan, Ashby was ashamed of how she'd misjudged him. Hearing about his childhood highlighted the sharp contrast to her own. He amazed her. And his mother… God bless her for what she'd done to give her child a better, safer life.

"What happened to your mom?"

Ashby knew she should take her hand off his arm, but their conversation had turned so serious, she felt a need to comfort him. Her question brought pain to his eyes and he suddenly covered her hand with his. Ashby couldn't explain the feelings that rocked through her. She felt guilty that she'd asked the question that brought pain into his eyes, and yet she was undeniably attracted to him. To the man she'd not realized he was.

"My mom…" His smile was full of love and regret. "She finally found a good man. A missionary, and she was so in love with…" Dan's voice trailed off and his eyes held Ashby's. "She found a man she could trust with her fragile heart. I had to relinquish the role of her protector to Jeff, and for a man who'd taken it on with serious intent as a young kid, that was a big deal. But seeing her so happy, I was pleased to hand that responsibility over to him. They were on a trip to the mission field when their plane went down."

Ashby gasped and tears filled her eyes. "I'm so sorry," she said, her voice cracking with emotion.

He traced his fingers across the back of her hand distractedly, almost as if he didn't realize he was doing so. "God has a plan. He's in control—that was Mom's favorite phrase. When things were at their worst, she'd look me in the eye and tell me that God has a plan for all of us. That He had a special plan for me."

Dan drew a deep breath and held Ashby's gaze for a long moment. Her breath deserted her.

"He has a plan for you, too, Ashby. And it's on His timetable." He lifted her hand and kissed it. The motion was as unexpected as the kiss on the stairs had been. "You don't need to rush your life. I think, watching you sometimes, that you're so focused on what you want, you can't fully enjoy today...." His expression turned solemn and he looked away as he stood up. "I think it's time for me to go."

Ashby watched him roll up the plans and slide them into the cylinder. They had just crossed into new territory. He knew it as well as she did.... He looked as conflicted about that as she felt.

Needing something to do, Ashby picked up the glasses. Her hands trembled as she carried them to the sink. She had all kinds of explanations for the emotions that he'd ignited inside her. The man was such a contradiction in so many ways, and she understood him now. Understood and admired him very much. But where did that leave them? Where did she want them to be?

He startled her when she turned around and found him standing there. "You're a good woman, Ash."

He was so near she could almost hear his heart beating. Or was that hers, pounding out a staccato rhythm?

"Some man is going to be lucky to call you his wife one of these days." One corner of his lips lifted and then he took a deep, shuddering breath. "You just need to slow down and wait."

He turned and strode to her door. His long-legged stride had him there within the blink of an eye, and just like that he was gone.

Chapter Seventeen

Ashby felt as if she'd been turned topsy-turvy and shaken. Up was down and down was up and she felt certain that she'd run into a few walls before she made it to work the next day.

"Hey, are you okay?" Rose shot her a hard look the minute she walked into the shop.

"Fine. I'm fine."

"You are not. Look at you. You look like you're carrying mail for the Pony Express with those bulging saddlebags under your eyes!"

"Aren't you sweet this morning."

Rose laughed. "Sorry, I'm tired, too. I was up late helping Max with some homework. Talk about making me feel old."

"I can only imagine. Did you get it done?"

"Finally. Math just isn't my cup of tea. Nive came in and helped us. That girl is so smart. Like you, trying to avoid my question. What's going on? The grapevine has it that Lance Yates has been asking questions about your relationship with Dan. Word is Lance's interested.

Ashby marked a price on the tag she was holding. "Lance..." she said. Handsome, Christian, a hard worker. She'd thought of the rather stilted conversation they'd had in the hallway at church a few weeks earlier. She'd thought then that Lance was the perfect guy to fall in love with.... Funny what a difference a few weeks could make. "He's a nice guy."

"But?"

Ashby's brow creased as she looked at her friend and lifted one shoulder. There were things about Dan she couldn't explain to Rose. Things he'd confided in her that she knew instinctively he hadn't shared with many people. How could she tell Rose that he might not want children? She couldn't, because she suspected that the things he'd suffered through in his childhood had something to do with this indecision. She couldn't expose that confidence.

He'd shared his past with her and then he'd told her they had no future together.

She'd heard the message loud and clear when he'd told her that some man was going to be lucky to call her his wife "one of these days." And had implied it wasn't going to be him.

Ashby knew God had a plan, and a timetable. But there were such things as detours. Was this a detour?

"But," she said, echoing Rose, "I'm in a big mess.

I'm falling for Dan, it's true, but it's complicated and I don't believe anything can come of it."

Rose's teasing grin turned to one of comfort. "God can work anything out, Ashby. No matter how complicated."

Ashby took her words to heart. "I know you're right." But the question was, would He? And could she give her heart over to a man who might not want the same things in life that she did? Could she sacrifice her dreams of a family for a man who might not be able to overcome the way his past was holding him back? God forgive her, but she wasn't sure she could.

And it might not be a question left up to her. Dan clearly had his own thoughts when it came to this.

"Trust Him, Ashby. Let go, and trust the Lord."

"I keep thinking I am, only to realize I'm floundering again."

"Believe me, I understand completely. It's much easier for me to tell you to trust the Lord when you're the one in the midst of the turmoil. I've had my share of moments and I'm sure I'll have more. But as I'm certain you already know, God is very patient and gracious."

Ashby was still thinking about Rose's words hours later when she was alone in the store. Rose had left for the day to pick up Max from school, having hugged Ashby before she left. The woman was a walking, talking blessing to Ashby, and by the time she'd left for the day Ashby was feeling better. She was just going to keep doing what she'd been doing and trust the Lord to show her the way.

When the door opened at four o'clock and Dan walked in, she felt such gladness inside that she couldn't deny it.

"Hi," he said.

"Hello." She glued her eyes to the computer screen, trying to keep her wits about her.

"Busy, huh?" he commented.

"Mmm-hmm," she mumbled, scanning numbers she was no longer seeing.

"Look, I was on my way through town. I have on my farrier cap today and I'm heading out to fix up a couple of Jack Newman's horses. I was wondering if you would ride out to my place with me when I get back into town. I wanted to ask your advice about something."

Ashby should have told him no immediately. "What is it you want to know?" she asked. She was amazed that she sounded so normal. She didn't feel normal at all.

"It's a secret." That trademark smile bloomed across his face, sending Ashby's heart into a nosedive. "You have to come with me to find out."

"Okay," she managed to say.

His eyes lit up and the smile grew warmer still. "Good," he said, backing toward the door. "Great. I'll be back."

Ashby knew she'd lost her mind. Straight up, as Applegate Thornton would say.

Dan bumped into a clothes rack. "I'll be back around closing time," he said, thrusting a blouse back into its slot before reaching for the door. She understood suddenly that he was struggling with feelings just as much as she was—or at least it appeared that way.

Ashby watched him go. It was as if she'd just dived off the end of a pier. The problem was she couldn't swim.

"A barbecue."

Ashby stood in the center of the newly cleaned concrete slab and surveyed the area. Cleared off, it looked huge.

"Yeah, to thank everyone for all they've done. Don't you think this would be perfect?"

Ashby walked to the center of the slab to put distance between them. Obviously, he'd gone home and showered before coming to pick her up at the shop, and as he had the day before, he smelled of spicy soap and a light, appealing aftershave that did things to her concentration. Thus the distance. Who was she kidding—she needed the distance simply for the fact that she couldn't think while standing near him. Aftershave had nothing to do with it.

"That sounds like a wonderful idea." It did. And like something the man she was getting to know—the man she was falling in love with—would do.

"So will you help me?"

"Help you?" The question took her by surprise.

He looked uncharacteristically sheepish. "Yeah, I figure with all that fancy upbringing, you could help me put on a great party. I don't know a thing about doing something like that."

Ashby had to laugh. "You mean you want a barbecue spread set with crystal and silver? Pretty fancy stuff."

He blushed. She actually saw the pink beneath his tan. *Adorable.*

"Not exactly what I had in mind," he said, his eyes twinkling. "But will you help?"

Ashby swallowed, feeling the lump in her throat. "Certainly." She spun away and studied the area, her thoughts spinning. "You want to have the party before Thursday?"

He came to stand beside her. "Is that asking for the impossible?"

She looked up at him and shook her head, as much for her sake as his. He wanted her advice. That was all. "Okay, let's envision this." She started to walk away again, but his hand on her arm stopped her, tugging her into his arms. She leaned her forehead against his shoulder and his arms tightened.

"Thank you," he whispered, and kissed her hair.

The tenderness of the gesture caused a sadness to fill Ashby, knowing there were so many reasons this might never work. It felt right being in Dan's arms. She closed her eyes and lived in the moment. There was a protest going on inside her head, but she let it go. Reality would return soon enough. For now, as Rose had urged her, she lived in this sweet moment with Dan.

As if sensing her sadness, he hugged her tighter. "I have another surprise," he said. She thought she felt his arms tremble and she felt a sense of loss as he dropped one arm, but felt happy again when he tucked her beneath the other one and started toward the barn.

"I don't know if I'm ready for more surprises," she said, fighting back a sense of longing. The moment felt so perfect. But she feared it couldn't last.

He laughed and rubbed her arm as he hugged her, then continued walking.

Once there, he opened the door and tugged her inside.

"All the way down here," he said, leading her to one of the stalls. "Ash, meet Gracie."

It was a foal. A gangly, adorable black foal that couldn't be more than a few days old.

"When did this happen?" Ashby asked, her voice hushed in awe.

"Last week. She was over at Clint's so I could keep an eye on her, back when I was staying out there. We didn't transport them here until this morning."

Ashby reached in and called to the baby. Her mother made a gentle snorting sound, and to Ashby's surprise, nudged the foal toward her. Ashby met the mare's eyes and wondered if they were kindred spirits. "What a proud mama you have," she murmured, running gentle fingers down Gracie's forehead.

The mare lifted her head as if preening, and Ashby laughed softly.

"She likes you."

"The feeling is mutual." Ashby glanced over at Dan. He was watching her and she had to force her attention back to the young colt, feeling as gangly and unsteady as Gracie. "This was a nice surprise," she managed, hoping it sounded less vulnerable than she felt.

"Oh, Gracie isn't the surprise. She's just standing beside it."

His teasing words had Ashby looking around. There

wasn't anything in the stall beside Gracie. Ashby looked at him with questioning eyes. "So are you going to pull whatever it is out of your hat? There isn't anything here."

He nodded. "Oh, yes, there is."

He moved past her and went into the empty stall beside Gracie. In a second, he came out with the bike he'd ridden in the race.

"I have been thinking about this a lot lately. For the life of me, I can't figure out why you wouldn't ride this thing. Why you wouldn't even get on it."

She gave Gracie one last caress, then turned and started walking out of the stable.

"C'mon, Ash, don't run away."

"Dan Dawson. If I don't want to ride a bike, I don't have to."

"Ash, you can't ride, can you? That's what it is."

Well, she couldn't be any more humiliated. He might as well know the truth. Ashby swung around. "No. I can't ride. And I can't swim, either. There, are you happy?"

He laughed and threw his hands up in the air. Of all the reactions, that was not what she'd expected. Spinning away, she stormed out of the barn and across the yard.

But she knew she was acting foolish and petty. After all, he'd shared his past with her, and this was a silly bike.

"Ash, wait. I wasn't laughing at you."

His words stopped her short. She knew him. She hadn't known before, but she knew now that he would never do this out of spite. The knowledge was certain, so much different than her opinion of him all those weeks ago when they'd been in the bike race together. "I know," she admitted with a sigh. "I overreacted. I'm sorry."

"Completely understandable," he said, pushing the bike toward her. "I've been puzzling over this for more than a month now, and honestly this was all I could finally come up with. You talking about your upbringing the other day planted this seed of an idea. Sure, you're a little stiff at times—now, don't blow a gasket! You've been better lately and I understand where that comes from now. But even that didn't explain why you wouldn't ride the bike. It finally hit me that people are generally defensive about things that are scary to them, new to them, or if they're hiding something. I took a chance that you couldn't ride."

"It's just so ridiculous for a grown woman not to know how to do something most kids learn to do early," she said.

"Not really. People don't always have opportunities to learn what some take for granted. I want to teach you to ride."

Ashby shifted from one foot to the other. She took a deep breath. "My mother thought bike riding was a waste of my time. Swimming too dangerous."

Dan studied her with an encouraging light in his eyes. "I'll teach you to swim, too."

"I'm almost thirty years old."

He laughed, threw his head back and belted one out. "You act like thirty is the end of the world. You can still learn new things even at that ripe old age."

Ashby blushed. She knew he was right. She'd said

she wasn't going to let her mother's insecurities continue to affect her life, but here she was, letting them do just that. "Then teach me," she said, planting her fists on her hips. "Teach me how to ride that bike. We'll talk about swimming after that."

He flashed that grin that made her toes curl up. "Well get ready, sugar pie. This is going to be one afternoon you won't soon forget."

It already was.

Chapter Eighteen

Ashby put aside the fact that she felt silly as she perched on the seat of the bike with Dan pushing her. The excitement was too great. She was learning to ride a bike!

She laughed as she glanced at him, jogging beside her, holding the seat with one hand and urging her to pedal. His eyes were sparkling.

"You can't steer this thing if you keep looking at me," he exclaimed.

She proved him right when the bike wobbled. "Oh!" she cried, refocusing on doing her job. "Sorry. But I'm afraid you're going to let go."

He chuckled, his breath coming in spurts from the exertion of jogging, pushing and keeping her upright. The man was in good shape. "That is the general idea, you know."

"But I get dizzy."

"That's just nerves. Hang on to those handlebars and just do it. C'mon, you know you can."

She was gritting her teeth, when suddenly he let go. "Wait!" She glanced at him as he continued to jog beside her. He was nodding his head. And she was riding the bike by herself!

She *was* riding—it wobbled. She had to put her feet down to keep from crashing. He immediately grabbed the seat with one hand and her with the other, keeping her from harm's way.

"What'd I tell you? You were doing it." He hugged her tightly.

Ashby's heart was thudding and the world was spinning, but she'd ridden a bike! For all of five seconds, maybe, but next time she was going to do it longer.

She felt like a schoolgirl. "I did," she said breathlessly. "And I'm not dizzy."

"You ready to go for gold?" He rubbed her arms briskly, like a coach getting his athlete warmed up for the next event.

She nodded.

"That's my girl. Okay, this time, since you have a feel for the balance needed, you're going to try it on your own. You don't need me."

Ashby wasn't so sure about that. Dan Dawson brought something to her world that she'd never known before. Not only did he add his own style of confidence, he provided an element of fun and spontaneity. Sure, she could have learned to ride a bike on her own. But would she have? Dan shared his sense of adventure with her; it rubbed off on her when he was around…and looking at him now, she realized how much she'd started to crave that.

"This is some shindig," Applegate shouted over the country band on Thursday evening. He saluted Dan with the chicken leg he'd plucked from the overflowing table of food on his way over to talk to him.

Dan watched Ashby, still amazed at what she'd pulled off in two short days. He hadn't given her much notice, but she'd done it. Of course, he'd never thought she couldn't. The woman was amazing. She was vulnerable in the most surprising ways, and strong in more ways than she seemed to know.

He'd never met anyone quite like her.

"You hear what I said?" Applegate shouted louder, and poked the drumstick at him. Dan realized he'd never answered the older man.

"Yes, sir. I think Ashby did a great job."

App nodded, his bushy eyebrows wrinkled up like caterpillars inching across his forehead. "That's a fine woman," he said, and bit into his chicken.

"Yes, sir, she is."

"A mighty fine hostess," App mumbled as he chewed.

"Yes, sir." Dan watched Ashby as she zipped here and there, making certain everyone was taken care of. He hadn't realized how this would look to most folks…as if they were a couple. But that was exactly how all the cowboys were taking it. Everyone, that is, except Lance Yates. The cowboy had been lingering around Ashby all evening, and Dan didn't like it at all.

Not that he had any claim to Ash, but there was just no sense denying that his feelings for her were far deeper than he was comfortable with. He had pushed for this relationship. He'd been obsessed to learn more about her, even after he knew how much she wanted children. Even knowing how he felt about having children of his own.

As he and Applegate watched, Lance stepped up and started talking to her.

"Competition," App said, glaring at him. "Thar's a man that knows a prize when he sees it. Ain't you gonna get over thar and stake your claim to her?"

Dan shifted uncomfortably. Ashby wanted kids. Lots of kids. The knowledge repeated in his head like a chant. "She has free will, App. This isn't the gold rush," he snapped as his temper flared.

Applegate grunted in disgust and walked off, leaving Dan to deal with his growing bad mood. It was true he was madder than a penned-up bull and spying Emmett standing off under a tree didn't help. Now that man needed a kick in the pants.

"What are you doing all the way over here by yourself?" Dan asked after stalking across the lawn. His mood had gone darker than a stormy night with a tornado coming. The fact that Emmett wasn't taking advantage of the opportunity this "festive" event provided added to Dan's irritation.

The cowboy looked miserable. "I can't help it, Dan. My insides are all twisted up and, well, look at me. I'm not much to look at, and just look at her." His voice went all milky and Dan turned to look at Stacy.

She was with the toddlers in the shade of an oak tree across the yard. She was a pretty woman, in a gentle, almost fragile way. Just then, she glanced at them.

"Emmett, unless you go over there and do more than stare at her, this is all the two of you are ever going to have. Your opinion about your looks isn't important right now." Dan was calming down. The frustration he'd been feeling about his own situation subsided a bit as he focused on Emmett and Stacy. "Look at her, Emmett. The woman likes you. She doesn't send those sweet little glances she keeps tossing your way to anybody else."

That got the man's attention. "You don't think so?"

"I know so, man." Dan grinned at Emmett. "Look at her...." She was watching the kids again. Emmett turned from Dan to Stacy. "There ya go. Watch—not me. Her. Now wait for it. Wait for it...." Stacy glanced Emmett's way and their gazes locked. "Bingo," Dan whispered. "What'd I tell you? You are the man, dude."

Emmett turned all patriotic, with his red face, white teeth and sparkling blue eyes. Dan glanced from the blushing cowboy to the blushing object of his affection.

"Now get over there and have a conversation with that woman."

Emmett mumbled something that Dan couldn't

decipher, but it must have been agreement, because he started walking Stacy's way. Dan watched as he came to a halt about four feet away from her. She turned toward him and he snatched off his hat and held it in a death grip. Just as Dan was thinking things were going right, finally the cowboy nodded, then walked away. *What?* Dan saw the confusion on Stacy's face, and Dan wasn't sure Emmett understood how hard this was for her.

It wasn't as if she needed some cowboy to toy with her like that. Even unwittingly. Dan resolved to have a serious chat with Emmett after the barbecue.

"You can't fix everything, Dan."

Ashby's voice startled him, and he swung around to find her holding out a plate to him. "I thought you'd like some food. This is your party, after all."

He took the plate because it gave him something to do. She glanced over his shoulder toward Stacy. "They are going to have to find their own way, Dan. You can only do so much."

"I'm going to have a talk with—"

Ashby's eyes flashed. "She is not your responsibility, Dan. She is a grown woman you have helped, but she is not your problem. If she and Emmett are going to fall in love, then they're going to have to do it without you orchestrating their every move. And both of them are going to have to come to that realization."

She had a point, and he knew it. "You're right," he grumbled. "I still don't like it. I mean, look at them. If he'd just come to his senses it'd be so much easier."

She smiled. "Aren't you the guy who's so sure God has a plan?"

"You're right," he said. She'd just sweetly put him in his place. "Thank you, Ash."

"You are very welcome. I mean, I get it. I think when I marry—*if* I marry—my husband will have to tell me that very thing when it comes to overprotecting my children. Not that I agree with most of the way my mother raised me...but I can understand wanting the best for your children. That's kind of how I see you now, protecting Stacy. Maybe not as a parent as much as a big brother. But she's going to do just fine, Dan."

He nodded. Ashby was right. But his mind had snagged on Ashby and the *if* she'd used in context with her eventual marriage.

That *if* bothered him. Here he was the one telling her she needed to wait, and now when she threw out the word *if* he got all bent out of shape. Again Dan felt as if he'd lost control of his good sense where Ashby was concerned. But he couldn't let his own longings trump hers. She deserved every good thing she wanted in life. She deserved a houseful of babies if that was her dream, her heart's desire. And if he couldn't give them to her, then he had to be man enough to let her get on with her life. A man who loved a woman would do that...and he loved Ashby more than he'd ever known it was possible to love someone.

Chapter Nineteen

On Friday Ashby rose early, left the shop in Rose's capable hands and drove into the neighboring county to visit some of her custom suppliers. The three separate stops were scattered across two counties, giving her plenty of time alone as she drove. Time for contemplation and prayer. Her life was a mess. She needed serious guidance from the Lord.

At the party the day before, she'd realized she'd lost her footing. She no longer thought clearly where Dan was concerned.

How could she have thought he was like Steven? How had she believed she loved Steven in the first place?

Steven had no heart; Dan's heart was huge.

She loved him.

Steven had been a selfish, cheating good-for-nothing. She now knew that Dan would never betray someone's trust like that. The mistakes from her past had blinded her to what her friends and the matchmakers had recognized early—Dan had the kind of heart women searched for all their lives. That was what drew people to him in droves. He was kind, trustworthy, giving, tenaciously patient and abundantly compassionate....

And afraid.

Fear was the only explanation she could come up with for his uncertainty about wanting children. He *loved* children, and they loved him. She'd witnessed it firsthand. Watching him with the toddlers had caused her heart to free-fall past all her preconceived ideas about Dan.

She wanted children. Even if she found out, after she was finally married, that there was a medical reason that meant she couldn't have a child, she would adopt. And she'd fallen in love with a man who wasn't certain if he wanted children.

He hadn't said he loved her, but she believed he did. What were they going to do? Could he seriously believe that he could harm a child? Was that what he thought?

Emotionally weary and disgruntled, she finally drove home, no closer to a solution to her dilemma than when she'd left that morning. God hadn't given her any peace. Her head and heart were still in turmoil as she trudged up the stairs to her apartment. All the driving around in the world wouldn't give her any answers. It was time to talk to Dan.

Dan was pacing his apartment when he heard Ashby in the hallway. He'd worried about her all evening. Ever since the barbecue he'd been trying to figure out how to tell her that he wasn't going to be bothering her any longer. But he hadn't come up with how to say something like that without alerting her to the fact that he loved her. He couldn't tell her in one breath that he loved her and in the next that he should never have chased after her in the first place.

"Ashby, where have you been?" he asked the instant he yanked open his door. Startled, she swung toward him.

"I was on a business trip," she said. "Are you all right?"

No. He rammed his hands through his hair and held back the need to pull her into his arms in relief, even as he wanted to fuss at her for not calling. *And why would she do that?* He had no claim to her. She'd just been taking care of her business—which wasn't *his* business. He was out of his element here. In way over his head. If she wanted to stay out past dark, that was her prerogative. She was a grown woman—whom he loved, cared about and couldn't help but worry about.... He was in big trouble.

"I'm fine," he said. Taking a deep breath, he struggled to rein in his frustrations, thankful she was safe. "I was just getting worried about you. I stopped by to see you earlier and Rose said you'd gone to see some suppliers. She said you'd planned to be home before dark. It's been dark for over two hours."

"I was driving around."

Relief was sinking in slowly. Calmer now, he realized she looked as upset as he felt. "You were just driving?"

She nodded. “I need to talk to you. Could you come in?”

“I think that’d be a good idea. I need to talk to you, too.” Dan felt as wobbly as when he’d tangled up dismounting during a bull ride and it had taken three bullfighters to get his hand loose from the rigging.

He waited beside her as she slipped the key in and unlocked her door. She smelled sweet as a spring morning, which didn’t help his wobbly legs one bit.

Inside, she immediately went around the bar into the kitchen.

He didn’t follow, choosing instead to keep the bar between them. He loved this woman, and now that he’d let himself admit it, he couldn’t stop thinking about it.

“Coffee?” she asked, starting to fill the carafe with water.

“Sure,” he said, needing the moment to get his wits about him. As she emptied it into the reservoir he realized her hand was shaking. “Ashby, you’re trembling. What is it?”

She set the carafe on the counter and turned to him, her expression pensive. “Why do you think you don’t want children?”

So this was it. She’d also realized the significance of their situation. He braced for what he had to do. “I’m not sure I’d be a good dad. It eats me up thinking about somehow snapping and—”

“Dan, you would never do that.”

The conviction in her voice sent a shaft of warmth through him. "But there is no guarantee. I have a temper."

She looked surprised. "Most people do have some sort of temper. But I've never seen yours."

"It takes a lot to get me riled up, but it's there."

She came around the counter and placed her hand on his arm. "Even if it is, you know how to control it. That doesn't mean anything."

It took every shred of strength he had not to give in, wrap his arms around her and forget his past. Forget how his father's legacy haunted him. "I think it'd be best if I stopped hounding you like I've been doing. Then you can concentrate on falling in love with a cowboy worth marrying, like you told me you wanted from the start."

She shook her head. "I can't do that. I no longer want to look for someone to fall in love with. Dan, I love you."

How could a man feel like yelling with joy and groaning with despair at the same time? He closed his eyes and drew on his determination to do what was right for Ashby. "That's not a wise thing. I can't make you any promises. My heart's not there when it comes to giving you your dreams. I should have pulled back the minute I knew how much you wanted children.... You're a very special woman, Ash." He touched her hair briefly, then let his hand drop away. "I wouldn't be much of a man if I told you I loved you and then told you I couldn't give you the babies your heart craves." He hadn't meant to say all that. To expose himself that way. But his defenses were too weak near her, especially since she'd admitted that she loved him. Especially since he could see it shining in her eyes.

"Dan, I've been driving around all afternoon trying to come up with a solution to this and I finally realized, children or no children, I want to spend the rest of my life with you. If you'll have me."

Dear Lord, he prayed desperately, *give me some help here. Give me some strength.*

He stepped away from her touch, backing toward the door. "I can't ask you, or allow you, to do that. You want babies. I thought by the time I found the right woman for me I'd have resolved all of my issues. But it hasn't happened. God hasn't given me any peace about this. I'd rather die than hurt my kids. And I shouldn't have put you in this position." He turned to go, needing desperately to get out before he folded.

"You wouldn't hurt your child or anyone else's," she said from behind him.

He paused at the door, but didn't look back. "You don't know that."

"Dan, stop. You were the one who told me to slow down and trust the Lord. What about you? Does trusting the Lord not pertain to you?"

Heart pounding, he tightened his grip on the doorknob as he wrenched open the door. "I've been dealing and praying about this issue all my life, Ash. I can't get it out of my head. If God gave me some peace about it, maybe I could reconsider. But for now, I'm not stealing your dreams. You deserve a man who doesn't have a violent past. You deserve better."

"You don't have a violent past. You were the victim. You were the one hurt. You didn't do the hurting."

"Don't waste any more time on me, Ash." He crossed the hall in three strides.

"Don't do this," she pleaded.

He hardened his resolve and closed his door between them, praying she wouldn't try to follow him.

Tomorrow, after he got back from making an early-morning cattle run, he would figure out a different place to live until his home was rebuilt. There was no way he could continue to live across the hall from Ashby. Not when the weak part of him wanted to break down that door and run back to her waiting arms.

At six sharp the next morning, Dan walked into Sam's with a heavy heart. He'd spent the better part of the night pacing his apartment praying for the Lord to give him some clarity.

He'd told Ashby to trust the Lord, yet she was right—he wasn't doing it. Where she was concerned, he needed unequivocal assurance that he could be everything she needed. He was a flirt, just as she'd said he was. He'd dated and flirted his way through life and had been able to silence the fears inside him while he waited for the Lord to deliver him from the pain. He'd thought he was in control of the situation until he'd run headfirst into love with Ashby.

He was going to need a strong cup of coffee before he hit the road. Maybe distance would help.

Applegate and Stanley were setting up their checkers as he strode into the diner.

Sam was pouring them coffee, but all three paused to watch Dan coming through the door.

"You don't look so good this morning," Applegate said. "Stanley, ain't that right?"

"Don't look good at t'all," Stanley agreed. Both of them watched him stalk to the counter and take a seat.

"Sam, I need a big cup to go," Dan announced.

Sam rounded the counter, plucked a paper cup off the stack and filled it. All the while, Dan could feel App and Stanley staring at his back.

"You got troubles this mornin'?"

Dan met Sam's shrewd eyes. "Yup."

"Women troubles?" Applegate almost shouted.

Dan heard chairs scrape against the hardwood floor, and the next instant he was flanked by the two old codgers.

"Ashby got you tied up in knots?" Stanley asked. His hearing aid whistled as he fiddled with the volume.

Dan wondered what had possessed him to come to Sam's before he hit the road to East Texas.

"Yup. I'm in a mess, fellows," he admitted, knowing full well that he wouldn't hear the end of this anytime soon.

Applegate nodded solemnly. "It's about time. I been wonderin' when you were gonna wake up and smell the coffee," he said.

Dan needed some help here, and the Lord hadn't given him much peace about anything. "What do you mean?"

"We been a-wonderin' when the love bug was going ta hit you two. Y'all been dancing around each other fer a year now. That's why I told ya at the barbecue you needed to get your act right before someone else stole your woman."

"That is sure-nuff the truth," Sam said. "So talk. Why the long face?"

Applegate and Stanley huddled close.

"Well," Dan said, not believing that he was about to ask them for advice. "She wants kids right away and I don't think I'm going to have any of my own. I don't think I can—" He stopped himself before telling them of his troubled past.

"Sure you can," Sam said.

"There are things about me y'all don't know."

"What? That you're scared ta have kids?"

Dan looked sharply at Stanley. "What makes you say that?"

Applegate leaned toward him. "Question is what makes you think it? Them ladies at the shelter is always talkin' about what a good daddy you'll be. They say when you go out thar and help Brady around the place you are always patient and kind to them babies."

Dan took a deep breath.

"You know, the sins of the fathers ain't always the sins of the sons," Applegate said.

Dan's heart thundered and he met App's knowing

gaze. "But there is that chance." It no longer mattered to him that they knew. He needed to talk to someone. He'd planned to talk to Brady later that morning, but maybe these three could help.

Sam crossed his arms and stared hard. "You cain't sit thar and seriously tell us that you are afraid to have kids 'cause you think you could *hurt* them like yor pa hurt you."

Dan looked at each man. "How do y'all know about my dad?"

"We might be old as the hills, but we ain't blind," Sam said.

Applegate grumbled. "We been sittin' in that thar window playin' checkers fer years. We wuz here the day that van pulled in and them sweet women got off looking like Mule Hollow was their last great hope. And we been watching you come and go down thar at that candy store like clockwork ever since they opened."

Sam and Stanley were nodding in agreement.

Stanley cleared his throat. "We watch you at church, too. You got an extra burden fer them women. We kin see it in yer eyes."

Applegate slapped the counter. "We put two and two together. Until jest a second ago we didn't know fer shore that our hunch was right. But now we do. And if thar is one thang we know, you ain't the kind of man who would put pain in a woman's eyes like we seen in them ladies' eyes when they got to Mule Hollow."

"'At's right," Sam snapped. "You are a good man,

Dan Dawson. The kind of man 'at gets their eyes ta shinin'."

Dan's chest tightened. In his heart he believed he was a good man. That he was a godly man. "Why can't I feel confident that I'd be a good father?" he asked, his words quiet. Stan and App heard them despite their hearing problems. Both men reached out and clapped him on the shoulder. Sam did, too.

"Satan will bring a good man down with any lie he can make him believe," Applegate stated.

"The good book says, 'As in water answereth to face, so the heart of man to man,'" Stanley murmured.

"'At means like water reflects a face, so a man's heart reflects the man," Applegate said. "Just so you know."

Dan smiled at that. First time since yesterday. God had made him a new heart years ago, when he'd asked the Lord to come and dwell in him.

"You might have had a sorry sodbuster to call a dad here on earth, son, but you are now a child of the king. And that's what counts," Stanley said.

"Do you love her?" Sam asked.

Dan nodded. "I do. With all my heart. I haven't actually told her. I told her I couldn't see her anymore."

"Then what are you sittin' in here with us fer?" Applegate bellowed. "Why ain't ya over thar knockin' on her door?"

"Yeah," Stanley said. "Go on, get over thar and tell her you was jest mixed up, but we done set ya straight."

"It's not that easy," Dan said as he stood, dug change

out of his pocket and laid it on the counter. "Thanks for the good advice. I'd appreciate it if you'd pray for Ashby. And for me. I've prayed all my life for the Lord to ease my mind where this was concerned. That's all I'm asking."

"We'll pray fer you," Sam said. "We're gonna pray you come ta your senses and put us all outta our misery. Dan, you got a chance ta get married and have a passel of kids. Kids you can bring up to love the good Lord. Why in the world do you want to throw that away? The Lord is givin' you a blessin'."

Dan had no answer and headed toward the door.

Applegate stepped in front of him, his skinny chest bowed out. "It's almost like spittin' in the good Lord's eye, if ya ask me."

Dan hesitated, then sidestepped App. "Thanks, fellas." He walked outside, pausing to stare across the street at Ashby's store. She'd be at work in a couple of hours. He wondered how she was. Wondered if Applegate was right—was Ashby his miracle and he was spitting in God's eye by holding out for iron-clad clarity?

Chapter Twenty

Ashby was sweeping the plank sidewalk in front of her shop, watching each car and truck turn onto Main Street. She'd spent a long night tossing and turning. And praying.

She loved Dan. How could she fix this? What if he didn't come to his senses? She was upset with him. How could he tell her to trust the Lord, and yet he didn't? How could he tell her all that beautiful stuff about his mother and yet he was destroying her every wish and hope for him by giving in to a completely irrational fear? Yet she couldn't judge him on that. She hadn't been there. Her childhood had been a fairy tale in comparison to his. While she'd been complaining about dressing up and not being taught to ride a bike, he'd been suffering at the hands of a monster.... She blinked back tears as her anger flared toward his father. Taking a deep breath, she said yet another prayer for Dan. And looked longingly down the street wishing he would materialize.

She was about to go inside when she saw Emmett striding across the street toward the candy store. When he reached her, he stopped.

"Hi, Ashby. Nice day."

She smiled. "Yes, it's a real nice day. Are you okay?" Up close she could see beads of perspiration on his forehead. It wasn't even ten o'clock, and though Texas summers were hot even at this hour, Ashby didn't think that was his problem.

"Dan tells me I need to talk to Stacy more, but I'm not the best in the world at polite conversation."

"You're doing well right now."

He smiled sheepishly. "Nah, it's Stacy I get all tongue-tied around." He nudged a pebble with his boot. "I'd wait a lifetime to have her love me if I had to. But Dan tells me I need to make a move. That I need to take it slow and easy, but keep upping her trust level."

Ashby could visualize Dan's handsome face, all earnest and sure as he encouraged Emmett. She'd fallen in love with that side of him. He was a remarkable man. Not at all the man she'd first thought. "I think that's sound advice," she said.

Emmett nodded. "Dan's a good man."

Ashby met Emmett's penetrating gaze. "Yes, he is."

"Well, I'm gonna go in here. You have a nice day." He tipped his hat and strode toward the candy store. Ashby took a deep breath, then said a prayer for him and Stacy. With Stacy's past it might take a little while, but Emmett was all in.

How about you? Are you all in, Ashby?

Stacy could be a fortunate woman. Only time would tell. For Emmett's sake, Ashby prayed he'd succeed.

Ashby loved Dan. He hadn't said he loved her. He'd never made her any promises. But she knew suddenly that she was in. All in. As Lacy and the gang had told her before, if it was in God's plan for her to have children, she would. In *God's* time. Her heart hurt at the possibility that children weren't in His plan for her. Emmett had said he'd wait a lifetime for Stacy to love him…that was how she felt about Dan. God had finally sent her an answer through the shy cowboy. She would wait patiently for Dan to heal. She would show him how much he meant to her.

She took a steadying breath and placed her trust at the throne. Like Emmett, she was just going to have to put her love and her faith out there and see if her dreams came true.

Taking one last look down the street, she went inside the shop. She had work to do.

Her love life might be in shambles, but that didn't stop the world from turning. God was in control; she was going to stop fighting Him over it.

She'd just opened the door when she heard the bawling of cattle and looked down the road. Dan's truck was coming her way. He was pulling a trailer packed with cattle who were making all kinds of noise.

Her heart was galloping as Dan came to a halt in the middle of the street. He jumped out of the cab almost before the wheels stopped turning.

"I am a selfish man, Ashby Templeton. And an incorrigible flirt. And I've been as blind as they come for the last few weeks. God sent me a miracle and I almost turned you away."

Ashby expected him to halt at the sidewalk, but he didn't. He kept right on coming. One minute he was talking, and the next he'd enveloped her in a hug and lifted her off the ground. "This is me, Ashby," he said against her ear. "I'm all of those things. You told me you loved me and I didn't know what to say. I got over an hour down the road and something three very wise men told me this morning finally got through to me. I didn't think I was good enough for you. Or that I would be a good father."

"You'll be the best father ever."

"I want to be more than anything. But like they said—" he nodded toward the diner where three sweet men could be seen peering through the open door "—I have a responsibility to live up to. I can wipe away the past by bringing my babies up in a home with a dad and a mother who love them and the Lord. The fellas reminded me that Satan is the master deceiver…and I finally realized I was letting him make a fool of me by keeping me from grabbing on to God's blessings. You are my blessing. Oh, Ash, I was a certifiable fool. Please say it again. Please tell me you love me."

Ashby laughed and wrapped her arms around his neck. "I love you. And you are no fool. There's no point in slowing down life, though, unless I get to enjoy it with you."

He pulled back and looked deep into her eyes. "You sure about that?"

She nodded, knowing in her heart that none of her past experiences mattered. Dan was a man of substance and fun, all wrapped up behind that beautiful smile.

"Well, darlin'," he drawled as he lowered his head toward her. "Will you marry me?"

She sighed against his lips. "In a heartbeat."

Down the sidewalk, above the bawling of the cattle, Ashby heard a cheer.

"It's about time," Esther Mae called.

They turned to find Ashby's favorite ladies standing outside of Heavenly Inspirations, and the gals from the candy store stood watching, too. Ashby had come to Mule Hollow because she thought her time was running out. What she'd found was that it was just beginning.

She looked up at Dan. "Yes, it is," she said, laughing.

"You got that right, darlin'," he said, then kissed her.

And in his arms, Ashby knew she'd found her place.

The place where all her dreams would come true.

* * * * *

A gal with Hollywood dreams meets the man of her dreams right in Mule Hollow in THE COWBOY TAKES A BRIDE, coming from Love Inspired in July 2008.

Dear Readers,

Thank you for reading *Her Baby Dreams.* I hope you've enjoyed spending time in Mule Hollow with me and the gang!

I loved writing Ashby Templeton and Dan Dawson's love story. Like Dan, I believe with all my heart that nothing in our lives is wasted if we use it for God's glory. Whether it's something joyous, something painful, a horrible injustice done to us or some terrible mistake we've made in our past—God has a purpose for you and for me. Our past makes us into who we are today, and if we lean on God, all things are possible. We can utilize our experiences to fulfill our calling in a way uniquely our own. I love verse 1 Corinthians 7:7, "Each man has his own gift from God; one has this gift, another has that."

Dan Dawson's past gave him a heart for at-risk women, and his own experiences and natural personality led him to help in his seemingly shallow way. Maybe I was stretching it a bit, but I loved writing this big flirt's story and watching Ashby fall in love with him. I hope I gave you a few hours of entertainment, as well, maybe even a chuckle or two.

Until next time, live, laugh and seek God's purpose for your life with all your heart.

Debra Clopton

P.S. I hope you'll join me back in Mule Hollow in July for *The Cowboy Takes a Bride,* when Hollywood dreams and small-town dreams collide!

QUESTIONS FOR DISCUSSION

1. Discuss all the reasons why stepping out of her comfort zone during the pig scramble was a positive action for Ashby. Share an experience with the group that you may have had while daring to step out of your comfort zone.

2. Dan didn't mean to cause Ashby to make a bad impression on all the eligible cowboys when she first came to town, but he did. How did he try to fix the problem? Given all you eventually learned about Dan, were his actions realistic?

3. As a young child trying to make his mother smile, Dan realized he could use his playful personality to make others feel better. I loved creating Dan's character. Discuss the aspects of his life that shaped his character.

4. Dan realized at the end of *Her Baby Dreams* that he was letting Satan deceive him with fear and insecurities from his past. How? Have you let or are you letting the "master of deception" keep you away from God's blessings? How?

5. Ashby's childhood was one of privilege. It was very different from Dan's life, yet she had her own

problems. How did her home life affect the choices she made in adulthood?

6. Ashby's mother and Dan's mother each had an impact upon their child's life but in very different ways. Discuss the differences between these two women and what they thought was important.

7. What kinds of values do you want to instill in your children? What do you hold important in your life that might have a negative effect on your child? A positive one?

8. Dan tried to leave his past and his ministry behind, but when No Place Like Home moved into town, he felt that call again. Do you believe we each end up where God wants us? Do you believe God is in control of your life?

9. Have you ever felt as if God was ignoring your prayers? Ashby and Dan each believed that God was ignoring them. What did Dan want most? What did Ashby want most? Does it seem God ignores you at times? Why? Do you think He was ignoring Ashby and Dan? What lessons was He actually teaching them?

10. Ashby fell in love with Dan, a man who wasn't sure if he could overcome the deep emotional scars that

made him afraid to become a father. What sacrifices were they each willing to make for the other in the end? What are your thoughts on this? What does the Bible teach?

11. Rose told Ashby that it was much easier to tell someone else to trust the Lord than to do it. Do you find this to be true? The Bible says in Hebrews 11:1, "Faith is being sure of what we hope for and certain of what we do not see." Why do you think sometimes even those of us who believe this verse and claim it as our own sometimes struggle in the midst of turmoil to trust that God is still in control?

12. Dan had prayed all his life that the Lord would take away his fear of fathering children. Were his fears valid? Why and why not?

13. As I wrote *Her Baby Dreams* I was reminded that God loves me. And He loves you, too. In verse after verse He reminds us not only that He loves us but also not to be afraid, that He is with us always. Why do you think He repeats these messages so many times?

14. Did you identify with any of the characters? If you answered yes, would you like to share with the others in the reader group? If you enjoyed *Her Baby Dreams,* what did you like the most?

15. Here are a few of the Bible verses that inspired the plotting of this book. Read and discuss how they helped form the characters in *Her Baby Dreams*.

- Galatians 5:6, "The only thing that counts is faith expressing itself in love."
- Romans 8:25, "If we hope for what we do not have, we wait for it patiently."
- Proverbs 3:5, "Trust in the Lord with all your heart and lean not on your own understanding."

TITLES AVAILABLE NEXT MONTH

Don't miss these four stories in May

TO LOVE AGAIN by Bonnie K. Winn
A Rosewood, Texas novel

Laura Manning moved her family to Rosewood to take over her late husband's share of a real-estate firm. Who was Paul Russell to tell her she couldn't? She'd prove to the handsome Texan that she could do anything.

A SOLDIER'S HEART by Marta Perry
The Flanagans

After wounded army officer Luke Marino was sent home, he refused physical therapy. But Mary Kate Flanagan Donnelly needed Luke's case to prove herself a capable therapist. If only it wasn't so hard to keep matters strictly business...

MOM IN THE MIDDLE by Mae Nunn
Texas Treasures

Juggling caring for her son and elderly parents kept widow Abby Cramer busy. Then her mother broke her hip at a store. Good thing store employee Guy Hardy rushed in to save the day with his tender kindness toward her whole family—especially Abby herself.

HOME SWEET TEXAS by Sharon Gillenwater
When a strange man appeared to her like a mirage in the desert, he was the answer to the lost and injured woman's prayers. But she couldn't tell her handsome rescuer, Jake Trayner, who she was. Because she couldn't remember....